ALLEN COUNTY PUBLIC LIBRARY

3 ❤ P9-AFS-386

"I'll never get married!"

"You say that now," Rafe replied, "but when you meet someone…"

Tess glared at him. "Marriage is all about providing a loving, secure environment for children. That's why a man gets married."

"That's why *women* get married," he corrected. "They're the practical ones. A man gets married for other reasons. Most men are thinking about love when they get married, Tess."

"You're talking about sex!"

ROMANCE

KIM LAWRENCE lives on a farm in rural Anglesey, Wales. She runs two miles daily and finds this an excellent opportunity to unwind and seek inspiration for her writing! It also helps her keep up with her husband, two active sons and the various stray animals that have adopted them. Always a fanatical consumer of fiction, she is now equally enthusiastic about writing. She loves a happy ending!

Kim Lawrence's fast-paced, sassy books are real page-turners. She creates characters you'll never forget, and sensual tension you won't be able to resist....

Books by Kim Lawrence

HARLEQUIN PRESENTS®
2123—HIS SECRETARY BRIDE (2-in-1)
2147—WIFE BY AGREEMENT
2161—THE SEDUCTION SCHEME
2171—A SEDUCTIVE REVENGE

Don't miss any of our special offers. Write to us at the following address for information on our newest releases.

Harlequin Reader Service
U.S.: 3010 Walden Ave., P.O. Box 1325, Buffalo, NY 14269
Canadian: P.O. Box 609, Fort Erie, Ont. L2A 5X3

Kim Lawrence

A CONVENIENT HUSBAND

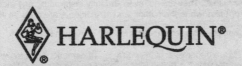

HARLEQUIN®

TORONTO • NEW YORK • LONDON
AMSTERDAM • PARIS • SYDNEY • HAMBURG
STOCKHOLM • ATHENS • TOKYO • MILAN • MADRID
PRAGUE • WARSAW • BUDAPEST • AUCKLAND

If you purchased this book without a cover you should be aware that this book is stolen property. It was reported as "unsold and destroyed" to the publisher, and neither the author nor the publisher has received any payment for this "stripped book."

ISBN 0-373-12209-8

A CONVENIENT HUSBAND

First North American Publication 2001.

Copyright © 2001 by Kim Lawrence.

All rights reserved. Except for use in any review, the reproduction or utilization of this work in whole or in part in any form by any electronic, mechanical or other means, now known or hereafter invented, including xerography, photocopying and recording, or in any information storage or retrieval system, is forbidden without the written permission of the publisher, Harlequin Enterprises Limited, 225 Duncan Mill Road, Don Mills, Ontario, Canada M3B 3K9.

All characters in this book have no existence outside the imagination of the author and have no relation whatsoever to anyone bearing the same name or names. They are not even distantly inspired by any individual known or unknown to the author, and all incidents are pure invention.

This edition published by arrangement with Harlequin Books S.A.

® and TM are trademarks of the publisher. Trademarks indicated with ® are registered in the United States Patent and Trademark Office, the Canadian Trade Marks Office and in other countries.

Visit us at www.eHarlequin.com

Printed in U.S.A.

CHAPTER ONE

'TOMORROW...? So soon...?'

Tess Trelawny closed her eyes tight in denial and willed herself to wake up from this nightmare. Minor—no, *major* flaw in this plan: she already was awake, awake and shaking as if she had a fever. Along with the deluge of adrenalin, blind, gut-twisting panic raced through her body. The leaden hand she lifted to her throbbing head was trembling and icily cold.

Chloe chose not to respond to the pulsating note of entreaty in her aunt's voice. She often ignored things which made her feel uncomfortable; besides, there was no reason for her to feel guilty. If Tess got awkward, Ian would back her up. Tess would listen to him; everyone did. He was the smartest person she'd ever met...and he was hers... A dreamily content smile curved her collagen-enhanced, red-painted lips...

'Ian is just *dying* to meet dear little Benjy.' Her lips tightened in exasperation as the pedicurist began to paint her toenails. 'Hold on a sec, Aunty Tess...'

The prefix invariably made Tess feel as if a generation separated her from her elder sister's only child, not a mere seven years. Now was no exception.

'This *stupid* girl is using the wrong colour.'

Tess could hear the muffled sounds over the phone as Chloe paused long enough to sharply inform the unfortunate young woman attending her that she had no intention of being seen with a shade that was so sadly dated.

'I was wondering,' Chloe continued once she'd satisfied herself the right shade was being applied to her toes. 'Has he got more hair these days?'

The question bewildered Tess. 'Why do you ask?'

'Well, you keep saying it's going to grow!' Chloe responded in an ill-used tone that implied Tess had been heartlessly leading her on. 'I mean, those little wispy bits are not very attractive, are they?' she elaborated sulkily. 'And they look gingery.' Her worried tone implied there were few things in life worse than a red-headed child.

Tess closed her eyes and took a deep breath...sometimes she felt the unworthy desire to shake her beautiful niece until her white even teeth rattled.

'Yes, Chloe,' she replied woodenly. 'Ben does have some hair now, and you'll be pleased to hear it's a gorgeous strawberry blonde.'

'You mean sandy...?'

'No, I mean strawberry blonde.'

'That's excellent,' came the relieved reply. 'And, Aunty Tess, for God's sake dress him in something half decent. How about that nice little outfit I sent from Milan...?'

Chloe's fleeting visits had always been infrequent, but during the last few months her acting career had taken off with several small but well received film roles, and the visits had become almost non-existent.

Tess was guiltily aware that she should have remonstrated with the younger girl, but the truth was life was easier without the stress and disruption of Chloe's visits. The problem was her niece resented not being the centre of attention and she didn't like to share that attention with anyone—not even a baby.

'He grew out of it.'

'Oh, pity...at least make sure he's not covered in jam or anything!' Chloe found it hard to accept that spotless, freshly scrubbed and sweet smelling wasn't the normal state of babies. 'I want him to make a good impression on Ian.'

If she were here right now, so help me, I'd strangle her! Tess's voice shook with suppressed outrage as she responded. 'This isn't an audition, Chloe.'

'No, this is the start of the rest of my life!' came back the dramatic, throbbing response. To Tess's uncharitable ears it sounded as though she were practising a line from her latest part. Abruptly Chloe's tone changed. 'Must dash, Aunty Tess...I've got a yoga class in half an hour, and I really can't miss it. You should try it yourself—I've really attained an inner harmony you wouldn't believe. See you soon!' The phone line went dead.

Tess didn't think she'd ever feel harmony, inner or otherwise, again as she responded urgently to the stomach-churning nausea and dashed up the narrow flight of stairs two at a time to reach the bathroom. When her stomach was quite empty she splashed her face with cold water. The face that looked back at her from the mirror was waxily pale, dominated by a pair of wide green eyes. The desperation and panic she felt was clearly reflected in those haunted emerald depths, and, even though speaking to Chloe always made her feel middle-aged, the person staring back at her looked a lot younger than her *nearly* thirty years.

Her feet automatically took her to the half-open door of the smaller of the two bedrooms in the cottage. Quietly she went inside. The curtains were drawn against the afternoon sunlight. She went to stand silently by the cot in which a small figure was taking his afternoon nap. He was dressed in dungarees—he was sound asleep.

The figure's ruffled blonde hair lay in spiky tufts over his little head. His face was rosily tinged and his long eyelashes lay dark against the full curve of his infant cheek.

Tess closed her eyes and a single tear slid down her cheek. Not so very long ago if anyone had told the dedicated career girl she had been that it was possible to love anyone so much it hurt—with the possible exception of George Clooney—she'd have laughed. But she did; she loved this little boy with all her heart and soul. Part of her wanted to bundle him up and run away somewhere safe, somewhere Chloe would never find them.

The sleeping figure opened his eyes, saw Tess and, with a sleepy smile, closed them again. Tess held the noisy sobs in check until she had stumbled out of the room.

The village was in total darkness as Rafe Farrar drove towards the stone manor house tucked behind its high walls on the outskirts of this picturesque little hamlet. A hamlet that was just far enough away from the popular stretch of coast to avoid exploitation and remain relatively unspoilt and sleepy.

He'd spent what most people would consider his idyllic childhood here. Since the death of his elder brother, Alec, and their father's enforced retreat to the Riviera, the only permanent occupant of the Farrar family home was his grandfather, an elderly but far from frail individual who was not adapting well to his belated retirement from the world of international banking. His relationship with his grandfather being what it was, Rafe could be sure of a *tepid* welcome from the old man, who didn't consider the black sheep of the family warranted breaking out the fatted calf for.

When he'd made the arrangements for this duty visit he hadn't planned on making the journey alone; a third party to act as buffer zone was always helpful when he and the old man came face to face. In this instance he'd been hoping to introduce the third party as his future wife. This had always been a situation with explosive possibilities, especially when his grandparent had learnt this future bride would have to rid herself of a husband before she made her second trip to the altar. At least he didn't have that problem now.

Thinking about the reason for his solitary state—for an individual not given to brooding or self-pity, he was catching on fast—kept the mobile curve of Rafe's sensual lips in a firm thin line. He was normally a scrupulously careful driver, but his dark embittered gaze did not on this occasion flicker towards the speedometer as his big powerful motor sped grimly through the narrow silent main street.

'Hell!' His language went rapidly downhill from this point as, with a display of reflexes that bordered on the supernatural, he only hit the dog that had darted out in front of him a glancing blow.

Still cursing, he leapt from the car, performing this simple task with the athletic fluidity that typified all his movements. He noticed immediately that his front headlight had not escaped as lightly as the animal. He kicked aside the broken glass that surrounded the tree he'd collided with. His unbroken headlight picked up the mongrel that lay trembling on the grass verge.

'All right, boy,' he crooned in a firm but soothing voice. With the careless confidence of someone who had never experienced a moment's nervousness with any animal—and this one was big and powerful—Rafe's capable hands moved gently over the animal's spare frame. The dog endured his examination passively. Rafe was no expert but it seemed likely to him that the animal was suffering from shock rather than anything more immediately life-threatening.

'Looks like this was your lucky night, mate.' Rafe scratched the dog, who gazed up at him with slavish adoration, beneath one ear. 'That makes one of us,' he added bitterly. He didn't need to look at the tag on the mutt's collar to work out where this jaywalker originated from.

This wasn't the sort of animal most people would consider worth a broken headlight. This was the sort of animal that looked mean, the sort of animal that was left behind at the animal shelter when all the more appealing ones had been selected. His off-white tatty coat didn't gleam, it was covered in an interlaced network of old scars; then there was the mega-bad case of canine halitosis. Given all this, there was only one person this animal *could* belong to. Even when they'd been kids she'd always managed to pick up every waif and stray within a ten-mile radius!

Trying not to think about what was happening to his pale leather upholstery, Rafe laid the old dog out on the back seat. Climbing back into the car, he headed in the direction of the picture-postcard cottage Tess Trelawny had inherited from her grandmother, old Agnes Trelawny, four years back.

Even if the lights hadn't been unexpectedly on in the cottage Rafe would have had no qualms about waking Tess up. Actually he welcomed the fact he had a legitimate reason to yell at someone—tonight he *really* wanted to yell! And with Tess he didn't have to fret about delicate female sensitivities; she was as tough as old boots and well able to give as good as she got. The more he thought about it, the happier he felt about his enforced detour.

Arms full of damp, smelly dog, he gave the kitchen door a belligerent kick. It opened of its own accord with a horror-movie series of loud creaks.

'Your door needs oiling,' he announced, stepping over the well-lit threshold.

It wasn't just the bright light that made him blink and recoil in shock, it was the disordered state of the room. For some reason the entire contents of the kitchen cupboards seemed to be stacked in haphazard piles all around the room.

'My God!' he ejaculated. 'Has there been a break-in?' He voiced the first most likely possibility that came to mind.

The shortish, slim figure, dressed incongruously in a cotton jersey nightshirt and yellow rubber gloves—a fashion statement this ensemble was not—ignored this question completely.

Tess rose in some agitation from her crouched position in front of one of the empty kitchen cupboards and rushed forward.

'Baggins!' she shrieked huskily. 'What have you done to him?' she demanded indignantly of Rafe.

'Why didn't you lock the door?' he enquired with a censorious frown. 'I could have been anyone!'

Tess spared her caller a brief unfriendly glare before her attention returned to the dog. 'But you turned out to be you. *Aren't I the lucky one?*' she drawled.

'Quit that!' he rapped out sternly as she tried to forcibly transfer the animal from his arms to her skinny ones. 'He's too heavy for you. Besides, the miserable, misbegotten hound is quite capable of walking under his own steam.'

To demonstrate this he placed the animal on the floor. 'I just didn't want to risk him sloping off again and killing some poor unsuspecting motorist.' He pointedly snapped shut the door behind him.

'Oh!' Tess's anxiety retreated slightly as Baggins began to behave like the puppy he no longer was. 'I fixed the fence, only he's started burrowing under it. You hit him with that flashy car of yours, I suppose?' Her full lips pursed in disapproval.

'Barely.' He noticed that Tess's narrow feet were bare too. Like the rest of her they were small, and though she was skinny it wasn't a matchstick, angular sort of skinniness, more a pleasing, rounded, supple sveltness...*all over*.

Rafe was unprepared for the mental postscript, only once the thought was out there it seemed natural to speculate on what was underneath the skimpy shirt thing. He cleared his throat and managed to drag his wayward thoughts to a slightly less tacky level—it wasn't thinking about sex that bothered him, it was thinking about sex and Tess simultaneously!

'Spare me chapter and verse on your lightning reflexes...*please*.'

Rafe, who was working up a cold sweat getting other reflexes under control, smiled grimly, displaying a set of perfect white teeth. 'Your gratitude for my sacrifice is duly noted.'

'What sacrifice?'

'One smashed headlight, and, yes, thanks for your concern, I did escape uninjured.' Testosterone surge firmly in check, Rafe found to his intense relief he could look her in the eye and see Tess, his friend, not Tess, a woman. It was a well-known fact that rejection could make a man act and think weird.

'I can see that for myself.'

'Why am I getting the distinct impression you'd have preferred it if I was sporting the odd broken bone or three?' he mused wryly. 'If this is the sort of welcome your guests usually receive, I'm surprised you get any.'

'I might be happier if I didn't,' she snarled.

'Thinking of becoming a recluse, are we?'

'You may be lord of the manor and the product of generations of in-breeding, but isn't the royal *we* a bit over the top, even for you?'

'I wasn't actually referring to myself.' He flexed his shoulders and rotated his head slowly to ease the tension in his neck. 'But what's a bit of poetic licence between friends?' Another shrug. 'And that was a *great* line.'

This drew a rueful laugh from Tess. 'It was, wasn't it?'

'Before you fling any more stones, try and remember, angel, that beneath this strong, manly *inbred* exterior there lurks a sensitive soul.' He took Tess's hand and planted it with a slap against his chest. 'See, I'm flesh and blood.'

Tess couldn't feel any evidence of a soul, but she could feel his body heat and the slow, steady beat of his heart. She stared at her own fingers splayed out against his shirt for what seemed like a long time; it was a strangely enervating experience to stand there like that. The distant buzzing in her head got closer. Feeling slightly dizzy, even a little confused, she lifted her eyes to his face...it swam dizzily out of focus.

Rafe looked down into her wide-spaced jewel-bright eyes and he hastily removed his fingers from around her wrist. Her hand fell bonelessly to her side.

He cleared his throat. 'And, incidentally, you may not be aware of the difference, but there is a big one between class and flash.'

'Toys for boys.' I really should have eaten something, she decided, lifting a worried hand to her gently spinning head.

'Insult my car, insult me.'

She gave a relieved sigh and grinned; she was no longer seeing him through soft focus. 'I'd prefer to insult you.'

'I thought you were.'

Tess gave a concessionary shrug—he was actually taking her nastiness pretty well, which made her feel even more guilty than she already did. She knew perfectly well that it was Chloe she wanted to yell at...only she wasn't here and Rafe was... Just as well he had a broad back—very broad, as it happened, she mused, her eyes sliding briefly to the impressive muscular solidity of his powerful shoulders. Her empty stomach squirmed uncomfortably.

'Well, Baggins doesn't seem to be holding a grudge,' she admitted. The undiscriminating animal's juvenile performance was obviously for Rafe's benefit, not her own. 'You naughty, naughty boy,' she clucked lovingly.

Rafe didn't make the mistake of thinking her affectionate scolding was meant for him. 'You always did have a novel approach to discipline, Tess,' he observed drily.

Tess sniffed. 'I'm glad *I'm* not a blustering bully,' she retaliated. 'I saw you being incredibly horrid to that poor man last night.'

'I thought you didn't have a telly. Not in keeping with your green, eco-friendly, lentil-eating, brown-rice life-style...?'

His amused scorn really got under her skin. How dared he look down his autocratic nose at her? It obviously hadn't occurred to him that she might actually miss the odd trip to a concert or the theatre that had once been an important part of her life.

'*Gran* didn't have a telly, I have a small portable, and just because I grow vegetables I resent the implication I've turned into one,' she told him tartly. 'Besides, you've room to talk. At least when I do things it's out of personal conviction.' Or in this case a desire to cut down on the grocery bill—fresh organic vegetables cost the earth to buy!

'Meaning I don't...?'

'Well, you didn't show much interest in saving the planet before *Nicola*.' Nicola, the environmental activist, had been one of Rafe's first serious girlfriends. Along with strong convictions Nicola had possessed—in common with all the girlfriends who had followed her—endless legs, a great body and long, flowing blonde hair. 'You haven't forgotten her, have you?'

Nicola had been a long time ago and in point of fact his recall was a little hazy.

'A man doesn't forget a girl like Nicola.' He gave a lecherous grin just in case she'd missed the point—Tess hadn't. 'That girl had boundless enthusiasm.'

Not to mention a D cup had she chosen to wear a bra, Tess recalled cynically. 'Some might call it fanaticism.'

She was distracted from her theme when at that moment Baggins' tail caught a pile of plates and sent the top one spinning towards the floor. Rafe neatly caught it just before impact.

'This dog's a liability,' he grunted.

'Insult me, insult my dog,' she responded, mimicking his earlier retort. 'Perhaps,' she fretted anxiously, 'I should call the vet just to be absolutely sure...?' She ran an exploratory hand over the dog's back.

'If he was a horse he'd be dog meat.'

'Not if he was my horse.'

'You sentimental old thing, you.'

'That's rich coming from someone who has his first childhood pony munching happily away in the lap of luxury.'

'Reasonable comfort,' he modified. There was a twinkle in Rafe's eyes as he acknowledged her pot-shot with a rueful grin. 'If you're really worried about the mutt, I'm sure the worthy Andrew would be happy to make a house call.'

Rafe wasn't up to speed with the status of their romance,

but it was well known locally that the middle-aged veterinarian had been sniffing after Tess since he'd bought into the local practice. Even though his acquaintance with that individual had been brief, Rafe didn't doubt that his estimation of the man as dull, pompous and self-righteous was essentially correct.

Tess flushed at the snide comment and her spine grew defensively rigid. 'Didn't you know, Andrew sold the practice? He's moved up north.' She knew what Rafe, like everyone else, thought. If he *dared* offer her any false sympathy…

Why did everyone automatically assume that because she was single, female and just about on the right side of thirty she had to be gagging for the romantic attentions of any half-decent male in the vicinity? Admittedly, half-decent males were thin on the ground, and Andrew had been pleasant company, but even though the only thing they'd shared had been the odd meal the entire neighbourhood, if sly comments and knowing looks were anything to go by, had assumed Tess had been sharing a lot more with him.

Rafe's upper lip curled. 'I always thought he was slimy,' he drawled insultingly.

'If it's any comfort, he didn't like you much either.'

Rafe patted the fawning animal. 'He's new…?'

'So are most things since you last honoured us with your presence.'

'You're still the same.'

Tess wasn't flattered; she didn't think she was meant to be. 'He's pretty second-hand, actually. He was Mr Pettifer's dog—you remember him…?'

Rafe nodded, dimly recalling a frail octogenarian.

'Nobody wanted him.'

'What a surprise!' He couldn't imagine there were many households that would be likely to welcome this ugly brute.

Exasperated, Tess pushed the heavy fringe of chestnut hair, which was overdue a trim, impatiently from her eyes and focused on Rafe's sternly handsome face.

'He's got a lovely nature.'

'And bad breath.'

'Well, Ben loves him.' From the way she said it he could tell that, as far as she was concerned, there was no greater recommendation.

She might be wrong—she didn't see Rafe much these days—but there seemed to be something a bit different about him tonight. She couldn't quite put her finger on it...

'Have you been drinking?' she speculated out loud.

'Not yet,' he told her with a jarring, reckless kind of laugh. 'Just the thing!' he announced, swooping on a dusty bottle from the wine rack. His dark eyes scanned the label. 'Elderberry, my favourite. Corkscrew...?' he added imperiously, holding out his hand expectantly.

Gran's elderberry! She now knew for sure that something was up! In other circumstances it might have nagged him to tell her what it was. Only at that moment she didn't much care what was bothering him, she just wanted him out of her hair so she could think...not that that had got her anywhere so far, she was reluctantly forced to acknowledge.

'*You're* not proposing to expose your discerning taste buds to gran's home-made wine?' she mocked.

'Not alone.'

'A tempting invitation, but it's three o'clock in the morning,' she reminded him, automatically consulting her bare wrist to confirm this statement and realising she wasn't wearing her wrist-watch. Come to think of it, she wasn't wearing much, she acknowledged uncomfortably, pulling fretfully at the hem of her washed-out cotton nightshirt.

She had a distinct recollection of waving her arms around wildly, revealing in the process God knew what! Still, it was only Rafe and it wasn't likely he'd turn a hair if he'd walked in to find her stark naked!

Three a.m. or not, Rafe, of course, was looking as tiresomely perfect as ever. It went without saying that his outfit was tasteful and expensive. It consisted of dark olive trousers and a lightweight knitted polo shirt—not that the details really mattered, not when you were at least six feet four, possessed an athletic, broad-shouldered, skinny-hipped, long-legged body, and went around projecting the sort of brooding sensuality that made females more than willing to overlook the fact you had a face that wasn't strictly pretty. Strong, attractive and interesting, yes…pretty…no.

'I know what time it is, I was kind of wondering about you…' His gaze moved rather pointedly over the disarray in the room. 'Do you often get the urge to spring-clean in the wee small hours, Tess?'

'I couldn't sleep,' she explained defensively, peeling off the yellow rubber gloves and throwing them on the draining-board.

She didn't much care if Rafe thought her eccentric, bordering on loopy; she didn't much care what Rafe thought at all these days. In her opinion success had not changed Rafe for the better. He'd been a nice, if irritating kid when he'd been two years younger than her.

She supposed he still must be two years younger, time being what it was, only the intervening years seemed to have swallowed up the two-year gap and had deprived her of the comfortable feeling of superiority that a few extra months gave you as a child.

Superiority wasn't something people around Rafe were likely to feel, she mused. He was one of those rare people folk automatically turned to for leadership—not that she classed herself as one of those mesmerised sheep who hung on his every word.

Still, although she often teased him about his old family name, he wasn't like the rest of the Farrars who were a snooty lot, firmly rooted in the dark ages. Traditionally— they were *big* on tradition—the younger son entered the military and the elder worked his way up through the echelons of the merchant bank which had been founded by some long-dead Farrar.

His elder brother Alec had obligingly entered the bank, even though as far as Tess could see the only interest he'd had in money had been spending it. She didn't suppose that his family had been particularly surprised when Rafe hadn't meekly co-operated with their plans for him. Since he'd been expelled from the prestigious boarding-school that generations of Farrars had attended they'd expected the worst of him and he'd usually fulfilled their expectations.

He hadn't even obliged them and turned into a worthless bum as had been confidently predicted. He'd worked his way up, quite rapidly as it happened, on the payroll of a national daily. He'd made a favourable impression there, but it was working as the anchor of a prestigious current affairs programme that had really made his name.

The job was tailor-made for Rafe. He wasn't aggressive or hostile; he didn't need to be. Rafe had the rare ability of being able to charm honest answers from the wiliest of politicians. He made it look so easy that not everyone appreciated the skill of his technique, or realised how much grinding background research he did to back up those deceptively casual questions.

Such was his reputation that people in public life were virtually queuing up to be interviewed by him, all no doubt convinced that they were too sharp to be lulled into a false sense of security. Without decrying his undoubted abilities, Tess cynically suspected that being incredibly photogenic had something to do with him achieving an almost cult-like status overnight.

'I think better when I keep busy,' she explained glibly. Tonight, it would seem, was the exception to that rule. Fresh panic clawed deep in her belly as she realised afresh that there was no magical solution to her dilemma.

Rafe's narrowed gaze objectively noted the blotchy puffiness under her wide-spaced green eyes. She had that pale, almost translucent type of skin that tended to reflect her every mood, not to mention every tear! He recalled how impossibly fragile her wrist had felt when he'd caught hold of her hand.

'I promise I won't tell you things will get better—they probably won't.'

Tell me something I didn't already know! 'You always were a little ray of sunshine, but the depressive traits are new.'

'I'm a realist, angel. Life sucks…' He pulled the cork on the bottle and glugged an ample amount into a stray mug.

'I'm so glad you stopped by, I feel better already.' Absent-mindedly she accepted the mug he handed her. 'This is actually rather nice,' she announced with some surprise, before taking another, less tentative sip of her grandmother's famous wine—famous at least within the narrow precincts of this parish and then for its potency rather than its delicate bouquet.

Rafe shuddered as he followed suit and decided not to disillusion her. 'What's happened to you that's so bad?' he enquired carelessly, refilling his mug.

'Still the same!' It gave her a feeling of perverse pleasure to see her sharp, sarcastic tone ignite a spark of irritation in his dark eyes. 'You always did have to go one better than everyone else, didn't you? You even have to be miserable on a grand scale!' There was a warm glow in the pit of Tess's empty stomach; she hadn't been able to eat a thing since that awful phone call from Chloe.

'*Meaning…?*'

'Meaning my simple life can't possibly be expected to reach the supreme highs and hopeless depths of yours.'

Rafe's dark brows rose to his equally dark hairline. 'You got all that from a simple, *what's up*?'

'You asked, but you weren't really interested!' she accused, waving her mug in front of him for a refill. 'But then why should you be?'

'I thought we were friends, Tess.'

'We were friends when we were ten and eight respectively,' she corrected, injecting sharp scorn into her observation. 'Actually, I didn't think you went in much for slumming these days, Rafe.'

There was just enough truth in her words to make him feel uncomfortable and just enough unfairness to make him feel resentful. Before she'd had the baby and left behind her city lifestyle they'd got together pretty frequently. Things being the way they were, he wasn't likely to visit home often and after the first few refusals he'd stopped inviting Tess up to town.

'You moved away too,' he reminded her.

'I came back.' And that was the crux of the matter. When she'd been a driven, goal-orientated career woman they'd still had common ground, but that common ground had vanished when her life had become baby-orientated. *She* felt her life was pretty fulfilling, but she wasn't so naive as to expect others, including Rafe, to share her interest in Ben's teething problems!

It was on the tip of Rafe's tongue to ungallantly remind her that decision hadn't been initiated entirely by a nostalgia for the rural idyll of their childhood. He restrained himself and instead poked a finger against his own substantial chest.

'What do you call this, a hologram?'

'I call it visiting royalty.' She performed a low mocking bow, blissfully unaware that the gaping neck of her loose nightshirt gave him an excellent view of her cleavage and more than a hint of rosy nipples.

'Got the latest girlfriend in tow again? Going to impress her with the family crypt or maybe the family ghost?'

Her soft, teasing chuckle suddenly emerged as she misread the reason for the dark tell-tale stain across the angle of his high cheekbones.

'Or is that the problem—she *isn't* here? A frustrated libido would explain why you stalked in here with a chip a mile wide on your shoulder. Smouldering like something out of a Greek tragedy…I'm right, aren't I? The girlfriend couldn't or *wouldn't* come…?' she speculated shrewdly.

At least theorising insensitively about someone else's problems stopped her thinking—if only in the short term—about her own!

Now he had a pretty good idea what was under the shirt thing it was even less easy to stop thinking about it. 'Is it that obvious I've been flung aside?' he bit back.

'Like an old sock?' she chipped in helpfully.

There didn't seem much point indulging Rafe's inclinations towards drama; she'd had enough of that with Chloe. He thought *his* life was a mess, he should try wearing her shoes—not that they'd fit, she conceded, comparing his large, expensively shod feet with her own size fours.

It was hard to feel sympathetic when the worst thing likely to happen to Rafe Farrar was a bad haircut! She gave his thick, healthily shining dark hair an extra-resentful glare.

'It didn't take a psychic to see you came here spoiling for a fight!'

Despite his growing anger, Rafe couldn't help but laugh at the irony of her accusation. 'I knocked on the right door, then, didn't I?'

'You didn't knock, you just barged in…' Quite as abruptly as it had arisen, the aggression drained from Tess. Feeling weak, she gave a deep, shuddering sigh. 'Maybe I just got tired of being patronised…? Has someone *really* given you the push?' Her wondering smile was wry. It hardly seemed credible.

'You find that possibility amusing?'

She found the possibility incredible. 'You must admit that it does have a certain novelty value. Look on the bright side…'

'I can't guarantee I won't throttle you if you go into a Pollyanna routine,' he warned darkly.

'I'm trembling.'

Rafe's jaw tightened as he encountered the sparkling

mockery in her eyes. He found himself grimly contemplating how hard it would be to make her tremble for real...and he wasn't thinking of scare tactics! What he was thinking of scared him a little, though. If he was going to vent his frustration on anyone, it couldn't be Tess!

'It might actually do you some good,' she mused thoughtfully. 'You're way overdue a dose of humility,' she explained frankly.

Looking at him properly for the first time, Tess saw that he actually did look pretty haggard in a handsome, vital sort of way. She couldn't recall ever seeing that hard light in his eyes before. The price of partying at all the right night spots?

'Then I'll give you a real laugh, shall I?' he flung the words angrily at her. 'The woman I wanted to spend the rest of my life with—have children with—has decided not to leave her husband!'

Tess's startled gasp was audible in the short, tense silence that followed his words.

'Does that have the required degree of character-enhancing humility to suit you?'

CHAPTER TWO

'You were going out with a *married* woman?' Tess didn't know what made her feel most uncomfortable: the part that Rafe had been messing with a married woman, or the part that said he'd been contemplating wedding bells and babies. 'You want to have *babies*…?'

Rafe, regretting his unusual episode of soul-baring the instant the self-pitying words emerged from his lips, dragged an angry hand through his hair as Tess, after visibly recoiling from him as though he had a particularly nasty disease, started staring at him with the expression she obviously reserved for moral degenerates. He resisted the impulse to unkindly point out she was no saint herself!

'I don't think I've got the hips for it.' He didn't understand why this sarcastic response should make her flinch. 'And just for the record I didn't know she was married until it was too late.' He didn't know why the hell he was explaining himself to her.

'Too late for what?'

Rafe scowled at her dogged persistence. 'Too late not to fall in love!' he bellowed.

He saw her soft wide lips quiver and a misty expression drift over her almost pretty features. Oh, God, not sympathy…*please*…he thought with a nauseated grimace.

'What are you doing?'

'I need to sit down, and from the look of you so do you.'

Tess looked askance at the guiding hand on her arm but decided not to object; she found that she did need to sit down too. She made no immediate connection between the half-empty mug of wine still clutched in her hand and the shaky quality of her knees.

23

Rafe was relieved to find that Tess's spring-cleaning efforts hadn't extended as far as the small oak-beamed sitting room. He pushed a sleeping cat off the overstuffed chintzy sofa and sat down with a grunt. The grunt became a pained yelp as he quickly leapt up. A quick search behind the cushion recovered the item responsible for his bruised dignity.

He held aloft the culprit, a battered-looking three-wheeled tractor.

'I searched everywhere for that earlier,' Tess choked thickly, taking the toy from his unresisting fingers and nursing it against her chest.

'Are you *crying*...?' Rafe wondered suspiciously. He didn't associate feminine tears or even more obviously feminine bosoms, of which he'd had that unexpected eyeful, with Tess, and he was getting both tonight. It intensified that vague feeling of discomfort.

Tess sharply turned her slender back on him and stowed the toy away in an overflowing, brightly painted toy chest tucked in the corner of the room. Scrubbing her knuckles across her damp cheeks, she turned back.

'What if I am?' she growled mutinously.

A nasty thought occurred to Rafe. 'Ben is all right, isn't he?' he asked sharply. A picture of a dribbly baby came into his head and he felt an unexpected twinge of affection. 'I mean, he's not ill or anything...?'

It occurred to him, as it perhaps should have done sooner if he was the friend he claimed to be, that it must be hard bringing up a baby alone. He couldn't be a babe in arms any longer, he must be—what? One...more, even...?

'Ben's fine...asleep upstairs.' The tears were starting to flow again and there was zilch she could do about it, so Tess abandoned her attempt at pretence of being normal or in control—of her tears ducts, her life...anything!

'Something's wrong, though.'

'You don't usually state the obvious,' she croaked.

Rafe gave an indulgent sigh. 'You'd better tell me.'

'Why bother?' she asked with a wild little laugh. 'You can't do anything!'

'Oh, ye of little faith.'

'Nobody can,' she insisted bleakly. The alcohol had broken down all the defensive walls she'd built up with a resounding bang. Without lifting her head to look at him, she laid it against the wide expanse of chest that was suddenly conveniently close to hand. Eyes tight closed, hardly aware of what she was doing, she brought her fist down once, twice, three times hard against his shoulder.

At some deep subconscious level that dealt with things beyond her immediate misery her brain was storing irrelevant information like the level of hard toughness in his body and the nice, musky, warm scent that rose from his skin.

'I can't bear to lose him. I just can't bear it, Rafe!' she sobbed in a tortured whisper.

Her distress made him feel helpless. Helpless and a rat! Tess was putting herself quite literally in his hands, displaying a trust and confidence she had every right to expect if he was any sort of friend. It made the response of his body to the soft, fragrant female frame plastered against it all the more of a betrayal!

'Lose who? Your vet...?' he prompted. He took her by the shoulders and gave her an urgent little shake.

'You can't lose what you never had and furthermore don't want! Don't you ever listen?' she demanded hotly.

'Then who or what have you lost?'

'Lost my inhibitions—it must be the wine.'

'Stop laughing.'

Fine! If he preferred tears, he could have them! 'Lose Ben!'

'You're not going to lose Ben,' he soothed confidently.

Rafe always did think he knew everything—well, not this time! Angrily she lifted her head; tears sparkled on the ends of her spiky dark eyelashes.

'I am. Chloe wants him!' she wailed.

Rafe looked at her blankly. She wasn't making sense at all...maybe she had an even lower tolerance for alcohol than he'd thought.

'I know Chloe gets what she wants,' he observed drily, 'but on this occasion I don't think you're obliged to say yes. You really shouldn't drink, Tess...'

'You don't understand!'

Rafe shook his head and didn't dispute her claim as haunted, anguish-filled emerald eyes fixed once more on his face.

'I'm not Ben's mother, Chloe is...' Sobbing pitifully, she collapsed once more against Rafe's chest, leaving him to digest the incredible information she'd just hit him with.

If it was true, and he couldn't for the life of him think why she'd lie about something like that, it was a hell of a lot to take in.

When Tess had taken leave of absence from her job as a high-powered commodities trader, he'd been as shocked as her other friends when she'd returned afterwards complete with a baby. Compared to that, the shock had been relatively mild when she'd walked away from the job she'd loved after a brief, unsuccessful attempt to combine motherhood with a demanding career and moved into the cottage she'd inherited from her grandmother.

Now she was saying she wasn't Ben's mother! She wasn't anyone's mother!

It was a good ten minutes before Tess was capable of continuing their discussion. Looking at her stubborn, closed-in expression as she sat with primly folded arms in the old rocking-chair, Rafe could see that talking to him was the last thing she wanted to do.

'Why?'

'Morgan and Edward were out of the country, some jungle or other,' Tess recalled dully, speaking of her elder sister and brother-in-law who were both brilliant, but unworldly palaeontologists of international renown. They might be the first people everybody thought of consulting when a prehistoric skull was unearthed, but when it came to a pregnant daughter they wouldn't have been high on anybody's list.

'Besides which they would have been worse than useless even if they had been around.'

Tess chose to ignore this accurate summing-up. 'Chloe was five months gone before she realised and absolutely distraught when she was told it was too late to...' Tess paused and looked self-consciously uncomfortable.

'She wanted to be rid of it.' Rafe shrugged. 'That figures. She always was a selfish, spoilt brat.'

Honesty prevented Tess disputing this cruel assessment. Her elder sister and her husband always had either indulged or ignored their only child, and the product of this upbringing had turned into a stunningly beautiful but extremely self-absorbed young woman.

'A *scared* spoilt brat back then,' Tess snapped sharply. 'She didn't want anyone to know about it; she made me promise. So I took her away.'

'Isn't that a bit...I don't know, Victorian melodrama...?'

'You've not the faintest idea of how weird she was acting.' Tess had been genuinely worried that Chloe might have done something drastic. 'I thought a change of scene, away from people that knew her, might help. I imagined,' she recalled, 'that after the birth she'd...'

'Be overcome by maternal instincts.' Rafe gave a scornful snort.

'People are,' Tess retorted indignantly.

'A classic case of optimism overcoming what's right under your nose. Chloe was never going to give up partying to stay at home and baby-sit. I can't believe you were that stupid.'

'Why?' she asked, roused to anger by his superior, condescending attitude. It was easy for him to condemn—he hadn't been there; he couldn't possibly understand what it had been like. 'You don't usually have any problem believing I'm an idiot!' She shook her head miserably.

'I don't know why I'm even telling you all this. It won't make any difference. The fact is, Chloe is his mother and if she wants him there's nothing, short of skipping the country, that I can do about it! I wish now I'd adopted him legally myself when she suggested it,' she ended on a bleak note of self-condemnation.

'Don't worry,' she added, slanting him a small, bitter smile. 'I haven't got the cash to skip the country.'

That was another thing that had been nagging away at him. Tess had lived a starkly simple life since she'd moved here, she owned this place outright, had no debts that he was aware of, and she must have made a tidy pile during her brief but successful career. Yet this place needed a lick of paint. In fact it needed a lot of things—not big things, but... And when had she stopped running a car? He couldn't remember; it hadn't seemed important at the time. But covering the primaries in the States had been? In light of Tess's distress there was a big question mark hanging over his priorities.

'I could lend it to you.'

Just as well he didn't know how tempting she found his offer, even though she knew it was meant as a joke. '"Neither a borrower nor a lender be,"' she quoted sadly.

'I can't believe you've fooled everyone all this time.' Rafe was looking at her as though he were seeing her for the first time. It had taken him long enough to get his head around the idea that she was a mother—now he'd have to unlearn something that had been surprisingly hard for him to accept in the first place.

'It wasn't intentional, it just sort of happened,' she replied, knowing her explanation sounded lame.

'You didn't just sort of *happen* to give up a great job you loved. You didn't just sort of *happen* to spend over a year of your life bringing up someone else's child.'

'I forgot that sometimes,' she admitted. 'That he wasn't really mine,' she explained self-consciously. 'And I know what I did must seem a bit surreal to you now, but it was never meant to be a permanent solution. Chloe didn't want Ben, she wanted to give him up, have him adopted. It seemed so awfully final. You hear about women who have given up their babies suffering, never coming to terms with the regret.

'I didn't want that to be Chloe ten years down the line. I thought it was only a matter of time before she realised, and then I suppose as time went on I lost sight of the fact I was just a stopgap.' With a choked sound she buried her face in her shaking hands. 'I was right, wasn't I? She has realised that she wants him. Only it's been so long I...'

'God, Tess!' Rafe thundered, banging his fist angrily down on a blameless bureau. A dozen images he didn't even know he'd retained of Tess with the baby drifted through his mind—she loved that kid and he loved her. Mother or no mother, they should be together. 'She can't just take him away from you!'

Tess's lips, almost bloodless in her pale face, quivered. The eyes that met his were tragic. 'Yes, Rafe, yes, she can.'

'Don't give me all that martyr stuff, Tess. You don't actually believe it's in Ben's best interests to live with Chloe, do you?' he grated incredulously. 'You know Chloe—the novelty will wear off within a couple of months and where will that leave Ben?' he intoned heavily as her eyes slid miserably away from his. 'So stop crying and decide how you're going to stop her.'

The callous implication that she was behaving like a wimp really stung. 'What do you think I've been doing? Whichever way you look at it, Chloe is his mother!' she reminded him shrilly. 'I'm just a distant relation.'

'You're the only mother Ben has ever known.'

Tess choked back a sob and turned her ashen face away from him. 'I've been so selfish keeping him. I should have encouraged Chloe to take an active part in...' The horror in her voice deepened as she wailed. 'He won't know what's happening...God, what have I done...?'

Rafe dropped down on his knees beside her chair and took her chin firmly in his hand. 'You loved him,' he rebuked her quietly. 'There's one person you haven't mentioned...'

Tess looked at him blankly.

'What about the father?'

Tess's slender back stiffened defensively. 'What about him?'

'Doesn't he have some influence? I take it she does know who...'

'Of course she does.'

'He's been providing financial support?'

'He's not around.'

'You could contact him and ask—'

'He's dead,' she interrupted harshly. 'He died before Ben was born. Chloe is getting married, that's why she feels that now is the time to have Ben live with her.'

'Who's the lucky man?'

'Ian Osborne.'

Rafe's brow wrinkled. 'That name seems familiar.'

'Ian Osborne the actor...?'

Rafe shook his head.

'He's got his own series...'

Rafe nodded. 'The medical soap.'

'Drama,' Tess corrected automatically.

'A canny career move on Chloe's part rather than true love, I take it.'

'Actually, she's besotted,' Tess told him gloomily. From their telephone conversation she had the impression that Ian Osborne had a lot to do with Chloe's change of heart. 'You're such a cynic, Rafe.'

'Better than being a victim.'

His casual contempt really hurt. 'I am not—!'

He was pleased to see the spark of anger in her eyes;

anger was way better than that awful dull, despairing blankness.

'Whatever,' he drawled. 'You could convince this Osborne guy he doesn't want a kid around.' With a thoughtful expression he drew a hand slowly through his thick hair.

Tess stared at him. Only Rafe could come up with an idea like that and make it sound reasonable. 'I don't think I want to know what machiavellian schemes are running around in your warped little mind. I need to do what is best for Ben,' she responded firmly, trying to sound braver than she felt. 'I need to do what I should have been doing all along, I need to prepare Ben to go live with his mother.'

If it was going to happen she'd have to put her feelings on the back burner and make this transition as painless as possible. And if Chloe and this Ian person made him unhappy she'd make them wish they'd never been born!

'You can't prepare someone to lose the only mother they've ever known!' His hooded eyes were veiled as she stiffly turned away from him. 'What we need is inspiration. In the meantime, will you settle for coffee?'

'I don't want coffee.'

'You need it; you're drunk.'

She opened her mouth to deny this when it occurred to her he was probably right. If she weren't drunk they wouldn't be having this conversation. If she weren't drunk his shirt wouldn't still be damp from her copious tears.

'Don't move, I'll make it.'

Tess, who hadn't been going to offer, retained her seat. If she hadn't felt so dog-tired she might have asked Rafe since when he'd made her problem his crusade. She already knew, of course, even if he didn't recognise the reason himself at least consciously. The parallels might be tenuous, but she could see exactly why he was so fired up.

Rafe had doted on his own mother; he still did. The reasons that had made her run away, leaving her two young sons behind, had been wide and varied depending on who you listened to in the small community—everyone had their own pet theory.

To say Rafe's relationship with his stepmother had been bad would have been like saying he was *quite* tall and *fairly* good-looking. A child of seven or eight didn't have the weapons required to prevent a clever, manipulative woman from alienating him from his father. These days Rafe wasn't short of weapons, or overburdened with moral qualms about using them. In short, Rafe could be pretty ruthless. Maybe that was what the situation called for…? She firmly pushed aside the tempting idea of letting Rafe have free rein.

A few minutes later Rafe returned carrying two mugs of strong black coffee. 'Do you take sugar? I couldn't remember…'

The small figure on the rocker stirred restlessly in her sleep, but didn't waken.

CHAPTER THREE

GROANING, Tess subsided weakly back against the pillow. Her head felt as though it might well explode.

'That wine should carry a warning.' The not unsympathetic response to her visible discomfort came from a point not too far from her left ear.

If her head hadn't felt so fragile she'd have nodded in rueful agreement. 'If I go so far as to look at that stuff again...' With a disorientated gasp she opened her heavy eyelids with a snap—actually, in her head it sounded like a loud, painful clang.

Dark eyes smiled solicitously back at her. Her disorientation deepened and the clanging got infinitely worse.

'*You're in my bed.*'

Tess tried to sound as though finding an extraordinarily attractive man in her bed was an everyday occurrence. She failed miserably to achieve the right degree of insouciance.

Her manic thoughts continued to race around in unhelpful circles without delivering a single clue to explain away this bizarre situation.

'*On* your bed,' Rafe corrected pedantically as he curved an arm comfortably under his neck and rolled onto one side.

Did that make a difference? She hoped it did! A quick glance beneath the cosy duvet confirmed she was still wearing the least glamorous night apparel in her admittedly largely unglamorous wardrobe. Tess felt anything but cosy at that moment but she did clutch eagerly at this small crumb of comfort. And Rafe was fully clothed; that had to be a good sign...*didn't it*?

A sign of what? a drily satirical voice in her head enquired. It wasn't as if Rafe had ever displayed anything remotely resembling interest in her body. Why would he, when he had an obvious weakness for the tall, statuesque type? His married lover was probably another in the long line of blonde confident goddesses.

When she looked at the situation sensibly Tess was forced to concede that it bordered on the bizzarely improbable that he'd been overcome by lust! A fact which ought to have cheered her up, but since when did being forced to face the fact you didn't have any sex appeal cheer up any girl?

Hell! I just wish I could remember so I know what I need to forget!

Unfortunately her amnesia only covered the problem of how, when and with whom—cancel the with whom, that was fairly obvious—she had gone to bed. The other awful events of the previous day were not at all fuzzy. Chloe and her betrothed were coming to take Ben to the zoo. Even Chloe had recognized—after a little judicious nudging—that she couldn't remove her baby son without a little preparatory work.

Discovering she'd done something she would definitely regret with *Rafe* of all people might confirm her irresistibility, but it would also round off the worst day of her life *perfectly*! No, I couldn't have...could I...? She surreptitiously searched his handsome face for some clue and discovered only a moderate degree of amusement, which could mean just about anything.

'It isn't the first time I've shared your bed, Tess—not by a long chalk, if you recall.'

Tess was surprised at the reference. Her tense expression softened. She did recall; she recalled hugging his skinny juvenile body to her own and as often as not falling to sleep with his dark head cradled against her flat chest.

The poignant image unexpectedly brought a lump to her throat. She'd never had a friendship as close as the one she'd once shared with a much younger, more vulnerable Rafe. It wasn't reasonable to expect that degree of intimacy to extend into adulthood, but it was depressing to realise how far apart they'd grown recently. If something was that good it was worth making a bit of effort to preserve it. Their friendship might not have thrived on neglect, but at least it hadn't withered and died.

She let out a tiny sigh and allowed herself to feel hopeful. If this time had been as innocent as those far-off occasions he was referring to, she had nothing to worry about. She'd have felt even more relieved if Rafe didn't have the sort of voice that could make something as innocent as a nursery rhyme sound suggestive.

'Is the old walnut tree still outside the bedroom window?'

These days women usually opened the door for him...except for Claudine... His eyes grew chilly as he recalled that significant door that had been closed firmly in his face. Pity it hadn't closed before he'd made a total fool of himself!

'No, it was diseased, we had to have it chopped down,' Tess told him in a brisk tone that didn't even hint at how upset she'd been by this necessity.

'Time gets to us all,' he sighed mournfully.

Her eyes made a swift, resentful journey over his large, virile person. *Sure*, he looked really decrepit! To add insult to injury, she suspected that even in this sizzlingly spectacular condition he was some way off his prime just yet.

'It doesn't seem right,' he continued. 'A Walnut Cottage without a walnut tree.'

The same thought had occurred to her but she didn't let on. 'You're not going all nostalgic on me, are you? If it makes you feel any better,' she conceded, 'I planted several seedlings after they cut the old one down. And in the interests of accuracy I ought to point out that this was Gran's room back then; so was the bed.'

The one he had shared with her had been a narrow metal-framed affair that would probably collapse under him these days, she thought, letting her eyes roam over his lengthy, muscular frame.

Who'd have thought that skinny kid would turn into something as perfectly developed as this awesome specimen? Aware that her breath was coming faster as her eyes lingered, she took a deep breath and passed the tip of her tongue over her dry lips. When she swallowed, her throat was equally dry and aching as if she wanted to cry—only she didn't.

It was all right to notice that a man oozed sexual magnetism; it was quite another to let the fact turn you ga-ga. Rafe had enough people raving on about his physical perfection without her joining the fan club! She looked up anxiously to see if he'd noticed her drooling display and saw his eyes weren't on her face at all.

'A lot of things have changed since then.' His deep voice was warmly appreciative as he continued to stare at the up-tilted outline of her small breasts.

He lifted his head and his eyes were slumberously sexy. Her breasts responded as though he'd touched the soft mounds of quivering flesh with his warm mouth. The startling image banished all rational thoughts from her head for one long, steamy moment. Nostrils flared, cheeks burning, she fought her way back to sanity.

'Some things don't change—things like your complete disregard for other people's feelings.' It was a whopping big lie, so to justify it she began to feverishly search her memory for some example to prove her point. Triumphantly she discovered one. 'Your family must have worried like crazy about you when you went missing all those times...?' Looking at it now through adult eyes, she saw aspects to Rafe's frequent nocturnal wanderings that her childish eyes had never seen.

'If concern is expressed by the vigour of the punishment, they were *deeply* concerned.' Something in his cynical voice made her search his stony face.

The memory of the bruises she'd once seen on his back when they had all gone swimming popped into her head. Suddenly all those times he'd refused to take off his heavy, long-sleeved sweater on a hot summer day made horrible sense. Everything clicked into place and she felt sick.

Tess forgot her throbbing head; she jerked herself upright. Outrage glowed in her eyes. 'He hit you!' She thought of Guy Farrar with his mean little mouth and big meaty fists and her skin crawled. 'You never said!' she began angrily.

Nobody, not her dimly remembered parents or dear gran Aggie had ever laid a finger on her. Her chest felt tight and her eyes stung. She knew now what should have been obvious to her ages ago: their efforts to force Rafe to fit the mould of a perfect Farrar had gone beyond the verbal chastisements she'd heard often enough for herself...they'd tried to beat him into submission!

'Leave it, Tess,' Rafe said curtly.

'But—!'

'You're hyperventilating,' he told her, studying with clinical interest the agitated rise and fall of her small but shapely breasts. So, he'd noticed she had breasts! It was no big deal. However, noticing was one thing, staring was another. He firmly averted his eyes.

Tess wasn't about to apologise for her emotional response; she couldn't understand his lack of it! 'I'm not!' she denied breathlessly. 'Doesn't it make you mad?' she persisted incredulously.

For a long time it had, but Rafe had no intention of explaining how much effort and determination it had taken him to finally shelve the resentment that had simmered for years.

Her firm jaw tightened and her smouldering eyes narrowed. 'I'd like to—!'she began hotly.

Rafe took hold of her hands and, inserting his thumbs inside her clenched fingers, slowly unfurled her white-knuckled fists. 'I can see what you'd like to do...' he remonstrated softly.

Rafe frequently thanked his lucky stars that his only personal legacy from a father who'd automatically raised his fist on the frequent occasions when his troublesome younger son had annoyed him was a deep revulsion for violence and individuals who used it to control those who were weaker and more vulnerable. He was well aware that all too often the pattern repeated itself in each successive generation.

There had only been the one occasion when he'd used his physical strength to punish someone else—actually there had been three of them, sixth formers who had been making the life of another fourth former a living hell.

It was a sad fact of life, he reflected, but some kids had victim written all over them, and bullies of all ages could smell fear. You only had to be a little bit different—different but desperate to be the same as everyone else.

Rafe had walked into the common room one day to find them holding the kid up against a wall taking it in turns to punch him. He'd literally seen red; a red haze had actually danced before his eyes. That day he'd rid himself of several devils, and got expelled.

The touch of his thumb against the skin of her palm made Tess grow very still. The odd shivery sensation deep inside brought a troubled frown to her smooth wide brow as, warily, her eyes encountered his rather dark, rather luscious velvety orbs.

She hadn't been prepared to discover this sort of intensity in the searching quality of his dark glance. Quite suddenly the quality of the tension that gripped her altered. If anything, this fresh, tingling jolt of sexual awareness was even more intense than before. It left her incapable of doing anything but staring dry-throated and breathless back at him.

'I know you're aching to ask...'

Tess ignored the melting sensation low in her belly. It was perfectly understandable—Rafe's low drawl was pitched at an intimate, toe-curling level guaranteed to bemuse, bewilder and befuddle just about any female with a hormone to call her own. Tess's hormones, after years of wilful neglect, were staging an ill-timed comeback. She was aching all right, in ways she didn't want to think about; it was all extremely embarrassing.

'But, no, I didn't accept your drunken invitation. However, I couldn't leave you asleep in that chair so I carried you up to bed.'

'I didn't invite you into my bed!' Fists clenched, she robustly rejected his gentle taunt.

Stomach lurching horridly, she glanced uncomfortably at the solidity of his biceps. It wasn't difficult to see how he'd carried her up the stairs. It was so easy, in fact, that a ridiculously romanticised version of this event was playing in her head at that very second. The only thing that was difficult to see was how she'd forgotten it...

'No,' he agreed with a grin that was slightly strained around the edges. The frequent occasions in the night when she'd cuddled up to him couldn't legitimately be called invitations—they could be called extremely...provoking, however, and they had been a reminder that, though his heart might be broken, his more basic bodily functions were still in full working order!

The enigmatic quirk of his sensual lips sent her tummy muscles into a fresh series of uncomfortable fluttery acrobatics. Tess ruthlessly gathered her straying wits and recognised that this was only half an explanation. Rafe had carried her up, but that didn't mean he'd had to stay—in fact if he'd been a gentleman the idea would have occurred to him!

'And you were overcome by exhaustion...?' she suggested tartly.

'I guess I was,' he conceded, not responding to the challenge in her eyes.

Tess permitted herself a little snort of disbelief. He didn't look exhausted; in fact, she decided crankily, it ought to be illegal for anyone to exude that sort of vitality this early in the morning.

'Trust *you* to turn out to be a morning person,' she grumbled.

'Not exclusively,' Rafe corrected her solemnly.

Tess's puzzled frown encountered the sensual, amused gleam in his eyes; a few seconds later heat washed over her as the meaning of his smutty innuendo hit home.

'You always did have an overdeveloped opinion of your own abilities.' She aimed for amused but tolerant and almost made it.

Rafe heard the *almost* and grinned as he defended himself. 'I've had some very positive feedback,' he reflected innocently.

Tess could imagine but she tried not to. 'I don't require references, glowing or otherwise. What time is it?'

He told her and with a yelp she leapt out of bed. 'Chloe and her boyfriend are coming this morning.'

'What are you going to do—roll out the red carpet?' he drawled.

His critical tone really got under Tess's skin. He made it sound as though she had a choice. 'I know what I'm not going to *do* and that is resort to covert dirty tricks and manipulation.'

'Have it your own way.'

She shot him a sweetly malicious smile. 'I will,' she assured him calmly.

'I don't understand it,' she continued fretfully as she pulled a motley assortment of garments from deep drawers in the heavy old mahogany chest. 'Ben *always* wakes up before seven.' She'd found that having a baby made her alarm clock redundant.

Rafe's hand shot out and he caught the latest garment she'd carelessly flung over her shoulder in the general direction of the bed. It turned out to be a flimsy bra. A passing glance told him his educated guess had been bang on size-wise.

There had been a plus side to his sleepless speculation: he hadn't thought too much about Claudine. An arrested expression crossed his face when he realised how *little* he'd been thinking about her.

'Ben did look in earlier.'

'*He what...?*' she snapped, stomping towards the bed, hands on her hips.

'I suppose he decided there wasn't much room this morning,' Rafe speculated, gazing at the narrow stretch of tumbled bed she'd just vacated. On impulse he reached out and felt the warmth that still lingered from her body on the cotton bed linen. 'He tootled off. I did go check on him—he seemed happy playing with his toys so I left him to it.'

She gazed at him incredulously. 'Didn't it occur to you he must have climbed over the bars of his cot?' She'd known for some weeks that the cot's days were numbered. Ben had been eyeing up the bars lately with a very determined eye, and she'd already foiled a couple of abortive escape attempts.

'And that is...?'

His laid-back approach was intensely irritating. 'Dangerous!' she snapped.

'Well, he looked fine to me.'

'I can't believe you just let him wander around unsupervised! He could have fallen down the stairs!' she cried out, her voice rising sharply in alarm.

'Calm down, there's a gate thing over the top of the stairs. I should know—I nearly killed myself trying to step over it while I was carrying you last night.'

Tess gave a sigh of relief. That was Ben's physical well-being sorted. There were other traumas. 'He must have seen me in bed with you!' she wailed.

'What has got your knickers in a twist—the fact Ben saw

you in bed with someone, or the fact that he saw you in bed with *me*?'

Tess recognised immediately that there was some merit in what he said, only she'd have died before she admitted it to him or herself.

'Like I said,' Rafe continued, a shade of impatience creeping into his languid tone, 'I hardly think the sight will have seriously corrupted his morals.'

'That's not the point, you should have woken me. Routine is very important for children.'

'Remember to tell Chloe that, won't you?' Tess flinched and looked so stricken that he instantly regretted his cheap wisecrack. 'I would have woken you if he'd seemed distressed. What are you going to do about Chloe?' he asked her gently.

He swung his long legs over the side of the bed and stretched. The light material of his shirt stretched taut across his broad chest and Tess looked hastily away.

'What can I do?' She did her best to resist the tide of helplessness that washed over her. 'I'm going to remind Chloe that this thing has to be done slowly, sensitively, with as little disruption as possible. In fact, at Ben's pace. It's not like I won't still be seeing him...' There was a tell-tale little tremor in her voice as she lifted her chin defiantly. 'He'll visit, I'll visit...I'll be his favourite aunt...' It wouldn't get her very far if she let herself wallow in self-pity; being an aunt would have to be enough.

'And you think she'll agree to the cautious approach...?'

Rafe watched as Tess's delicate heart-shaped little face screwed up into a mask of iron determination.

'She'll agree, all right,' she intoned grimly. Stern-faced, she picked up the bundle of clothes she'd selected *en masse* from the bed. 'I take it you can find your own way out.' Distractions she didn't need and Rafe could now be safely categorised under that heading.

'Shower...?'

Tess gave a snort of exasperation. It was a mistake to try the pathetic Spaniel look when you resembled more closely a sleekly muscled Doberman.

'I suppose so,' she conceded ungraciously. Halfway to the door she paused and turned back. 'I don't need to say that I'd prefer it if you didn't mention to everyone just yet about…about what I said…Ben not being mine. I got a bit silly…' Not to mention deeply embarrassing. She winced inwardly as she recalled sobbing pathetically on his chest.

Another memory attached itself to the coat-tails of this recollection: the masculine scent of warm skin was so real it unnerved her totally. 'T-To be honest, Chloe's phone call out of the blue…it was all a bit of a sh-shock,' she stammered.

A nerve in Rafe's lean jaw clenched and his nostrils flared. So much for supposed friendship! This little display of trust was just charming!

'You mean I can't run around the village with my loudspeaker…?' Rafe knew a lot of people, but he was pretty selective about the people he called friends, he always had been, and he trusted that select band implicitly. It didn't seem too much to expect them to return that trust.

Tess sighed. Perhaps he did have a right to act a bit miffed—she probably could have made her request a bit more tactfully. But the fact was she had more to worry about just now than Rafe's feelings.

'All right, all right…there's no need to get all huffy, I was just checking.'

'It may have escaped your notice, but you're not the only one that feels a little emotionally exposed after last night. Perhaps I should be asking you to sign the Official Secret Act, too.'

'Oh, I forgot about that,' she lied fluently. She wasn't quite sure why the idea of being the recipient of further confidences concerning Rafe's love life should make her want to run and hide. It had been easy to mock and be mildly contemptuous, even laugh in her more tolerant moments, about Rafe's numerous, shallow affairs. She couldn't see the funny side for some reason of Rafe in love, Rafe talking marriage...

'You make it sound so easy.' The flicker of torment in his dark eyes made her look quickly away. 'Forgetting...'

Tess decided at that moment she *definitely* didn't want to know anything more about the woman who had discovered Rafe's heart only to comprehensively break it.

'I didn't mean to be insensitive, but...' An intriguing thought occurred to her and she made a tentative effort to explore the idea further. 'Didn't you want to be alone last night? Is that why you didn't leave?'

'Regressing to behaviour patterns laid down in childhood?' He rubbed a hand thoughtfully over the short dark growth over his jaw. Tess had never been kissed by a man who was other than smoothly shaven; she found herself idly wondering... 'Sanctuary? I wondered about that myself...'

Tess, her cheeks a little flushed, brought her own line of *wondering* to an abrupt halt.

'Wouldn't it be something if I headed for your bed every time I needed a bit of TLC?' he mused, lifting his dark eyes to her face thoughtfully.

The thud of her heart sounded odd and echoey in her ears. 'Very funny!' she responded hoarsely.

'Yeah, hilarious,' he confirmed without a trace of humour.

When Rafe emerged from his shower Tess was in the kitchen having produced breakfast for Ben, who as usual was in no hurry to finish it. There was as much porridge on the floor as was in his stomach. She had stopped trying to tempt the baby to another mouthful and had returned to her frenzied task of refilling the cupboards when Rafe strolled in.

'Morning, mate.' Rafe, who could deal with the wiliest of politicians, felt distinctly unsure of how you were meant to speak to a one-year-old. He winked at the solemn-faced youngster.

Ben responded with a grin that suggested he wasn't quite as angelic as he looked. 'Seed man!' he cried, poking his chubby finger in Rafe's direction.

'Saw, Ben,' Tess responded automatically. At least Ben's limited vocabulary meant she was spared any embarrassing elaboration on this theme.

'Seed,' the toddler responded immediately. Eyes bright, he waited expectantly for Tess to praise him.

'Well done, darling.' When she looked away she saw Rafe was watching her with a curiously intense expression on his lean hungry features, which faded as he turned to the baby.

'I don't expect you remember me, but my name's Rafe. Or should that be *Uncle* Rafe?' he enquired, turning his attention once more to Tess. 'Can he talk?'

'After a fashion, but you might need the aid of an interpreter,' she admitted. 'You and Ben can decide between you what he calls you. My money's on complete nuisance...' she added softly.

'I heard that.'

'You were meant to.' She reached up on tiptoe to replace a casserole dish in a high cupboard.

Rafe found himself unexpectedly noticing the way stretching pulled her already neat, high behind extremely taut. Despite the fact that her clothes could have been designed specifically to conceal the fact, it was hard to miss the fact she had a good—no, better than good body. Dark brows almost meeting above the bridge of his masterful nose, Rafe reached over her head and took the item from her extended hand.

'Do you know that most accidents occur in the home?'

'Don't take that hectoring, lecturing tone with me!' Angrily Tess spun around to find he was almost close enough to fall over. Not content with wondering whether he'd catch her if she did fall, her wayward brain began to theorise about how it might feel.

A tiny sound of denial slipped past her frozen vocal chords. She was close to tipping over into outright panic as, arms extended protectively in front of her, she backed hastily up until the small of her back made contact with the wooden worktop.

The atmosphere was suddenly so charged with sexual tension that she could hardly breathe. He feels it too, she thought, staring in a bemused fashion into his dark, dilated eyes.

'Brekkie!' a small voice piped up severely.

The adults, both recalling with a guilty start that they weren't alone, looked in the direction of the small speaker. Simultaneously they both decided to ignore what had just happened.

'Good idea, Ben. Is this seat taken?' Rafe asked, noisily dragging out a kitchen chair with a stagey flourish and, straddling it, he rested his hands lightly on the back.

'Is Tess always so grumpy in the morning?' Now wouldn't you like to know? a sly voice in his head drawled knowingly.

With a confused frown, Tess watched his smile fade.

'Powige,' the child announced mournfully, dipping his hand into the goo left in his dish.

'He likes to feed himself.'

'He looks as if he likes to bathe in the stuff. Nasty porridge. Mush...*ugh*!' Rafe's theatrical shudder drew a giggle from the child.

Tess could see the beginnings of male conspiracy here. 'Last week it was his favourite.'

'Mush, mush, mush, *mush*!' Ben, his grubby face animated, shrieked loudly.

'All right, I get the message.' Tess sighed. She knew from experience that was going to be the favourite word for the foreseeable future. It could be worse, she reflected philosophically, and it had been when Ben had overheard the colourful expletives employed by the electrician who had fixed their security light. The entire mother and baby group now thought she swore like a trooper at home.

Mind you, that notoriety would be nothing compared with what was heading her way once the true identity of Ben's mother was public knowledge! Some people already knew, of course: their GP, the kindergarten head at the school she'd already put Ben's name down for.

'I like bacon and eggs.'

'No...no!' Ben bounced in his seat as he enthusiastically concurred.

'No means yes,' she felt obliged to explain. 'Actually, no means a lot of other things too. Mostly finding out what he wants is a matter of elimination.'

'In this case I feel sure that it means he wants bacon and eggs.'

'He won't eat it,' she predicted.

'I will.'

'You,' she announced in exasperation, 'are nothing but a troublemaker! Anyhow, I haven't got any,' she lied.

'Ah...shopping day.'

As if he knew about such things!

'And I'm sure you're a whiz with the supermarket trolley.' She permitted herself a loud snort packed with scornful scepticism.

'I was merely about to mention that you might like to add razor blades to that shopping list,' Rafe announced, ignoring her sarcastic interjection. 'Do you know that dinky little razor of yours is blunt?'

Bubbling with indignation, Tess watched him rub a hand over the intact dark stubble that adorned his square chin.

'It wasn't...and the reason it's *dinky* is because it wasn't designed to remove a dirty great beard.'

Ignoring the fact the dark growth gave him a dangerous, dissipated but not unattractive air—in fact some women might actually go for that moody menace look in a big way. Some women—the ones lost to all sense of decency—might even wonder what that dark growth would feel like when applied to sensitive areas…a breast, for example…even…?

Two bright spots of guilty colour apeared on the smooth curve of her cheeks. She glared with exaggerated distaste at the shadow on his jawline.

'I could have told you that if you had bothered to ask before you went poking around in my private things.'

'You want to watch this possessive streak…it's not attractive. I mention this only to be helpful.'

'In this mood,' she told him frankly, 'you're about as helpful as a hole in the head!'

'You're cranky because you're busy, stressed and ever so slightly hung-over.'

'And whose fault is that? I don't drink alone…' Which meant, as she rarely had adult company, she didn't drink full stop, which no doubt explained her rapid descent into her inconveniently garrulous state of the previous night…

'Admirable, I'm sure. There are some things I never do alone either.'

Nothing, she decided, could be more deceptive than the open, innocent look on his face. She thought it wise to rise above responding to the wicked earthy innuendo.

'But drinking,' he confessed cheerfully, 'is not one of them. I'll make us some breakfast, shall I?'

'I'm not hungry and I don't recall offering you any breakfast.' Her cheeks refused to cool as quickly as she'd like.

'I assumed that was a mere oversight.'

'No, a rude and calculated rejection.' Which he seemed to be coping with irritatingly well.

'You ought to eat.'

He subjected her small person to a critical examination. His expression suggested he hadn't found much to approve of. 'You're too thin.'

'Luckily for me beauty is in the eye of the beholder!'

Wanted, one short-sighted, sensitive hunk. A tall order by any standards!

'This could eventually work in your favour. I mean, a lot of guys could be put off by the notion of taking on a ready-made family.'

'I suppose you would know all about being shallow and selfish. Actually, I can do without men like that!' she told him with confident contempt. 'In fact, I can do without men full stop.'

With a mouth like that he somehow doubted it. Rafe had a sudden strong impulse to test his theory about generously passionate lips. You can't blame it on the booze now, mate!

'Is that what put your vet off?'

When it came to insensitivity, Rafe was right up there with the all-time greats.

'For the last time, he wasn't my vet, and, no, actually, it was something *quite* different.' He hadn't believed her when she'd said she *really* didn't want to marry him so she'd had to resort to the truth—he hadn't been able to get away fast enough then.

'Found out about your snoring, did he…?'

Something flickered in her eyes before her glance slid unobtrusively away from his. A speculative frown tugged gently at the taut, unlined skin across his broad brow.

How would Rafe react if she told him? Embarrassed, pitying…? Taking a deep breath, Tess lifted her chin and, pushing aside the intrusive shaft of self-pity, pinned a stoical expression on her face. Major shock, hold the front page…life isn't fair! She'd had plenty of time to get used to the idea, but sometimes, as now, it still caught her on the raw.

'I don't snore.'

One dark brow shot up. 'Want to bet?' he drawled. From where he was sitting he opened the fridge door with the toe of his shoe. 'Well, what do you know?' he drawled, turning a cheerful face to Ben. 'Bacon and, unless my eyes deceive me, eggs too. Free range, I hope…' He turned to Ben. 'Tess must have forgotten.'

'The only thing I'd forgotten,' she announced, gaining very little satisfaction from viciously slamming a cupboard door, 'is how infuriating and thick-skinned you are!'

'But you miss me when I'm not around…right…?'

She didn't pause to think about the possible consequences of replying honestly. 'Weird as it might seem,' she agreed tartly, 'I do.'

Rafe turned to look at her in time to see a shocked expression appear on her face. He found he could readily identify with the emotion.

'Which just goes to show how starved for adult company I must be.' Her attempt at making a joke of it didn't quite come off. I always did have lousy timing, she reflected grimly…

'I miss you too, Tess.' Wary green eyes clashed and locked with thoughtful brown.

'You miss someone to boss around,' she accused gruffly when the silence started to get hard to ignore.

'There aren't many people in the world you can be yourself with, warts and all.'

'You mean you've got a licence to be unconscionably rude and generally awful with me!'

'Here's to bad manners!' Rafe agreed, appropriating Ben's juice beaker to toast her with.

Tess tried to look severe, she tried not to smile back, but his good humour was contagious.

Rafe and Ben were halfway through the meal she'd grudgingly prepared—Rafe had even gone so far as to feed Ben several spoonfuls of his mushed-up version—when Tess saw the big shiny car draw up. 'Oh, no!' she wailed, throwing her hands up. 'They're here! It's too early.' Frankly, ten years hence would still be too early. 'What'll I do…?'

Rafe watched her agitated routine with a bland expression

and a quizzically raised brow. 'Slam the door in their faces...?'

'If you can't say something constructive,' she hissed, rounding on him, 'don't say anything! The place looks a mess.'

Rafe didn't see the relevance of this inaccurate comment, but he knew women seemed to set great store by a dust-free environment. 'It doesn't, but you do,' he announced with casual brutality.

Tess caught her breath. There was such a thing as stretching friendship too far and Rafe was getting perilously close!

'Here, let me.' She eyed him suspiciously as he levered his rangy athletic frame up from the chair. 'For starters, you can take this thing off.' Tess was startled into immobility as he calmly began to unbutton her long baggy cardigan. He slid it off her shoulders with a flourish.

He did it very slickly, but then he had probably had a lot of experience removing items of female clothing... Perhaps she should have forced herself to eat breakfast; she did feel distinctly queasy.

'Well, what did you expect?' she snapped tartly as he continued to look with obvious discontent at the simple slit-necked black tee shirt she wore underneath. She failed completely to appreciate how well it displayed her taut, firm figure and neat waist. 'Besides, I fail to see what difference the way I look makes to anything.'

'Don't be naive, Tess.' Rafe lifted a distracted hand and, with a brooding expression, rubbed it back and forth over his unshaven chin. 'Would you have turned up in your scruffy jeans for a big meeting when you were working in the City? No, you wanted to make the right impression and feel in control. Now is no different. I'm not saying clothes maketh the woman, but I am saying—and so will you, if you're strictly honest—that the right outfit doesn't do any harm. People like Chloe judge folk by the way they dress, the car they drive...'

'I don't drive any more.'

'I haven't forgotten that.'

Maybe his thoughtful expression wasn't significant. Maybe it was her guilty conscience making her see things that weren't there.

'If you look good you'll be sending a subliminal message to Chloe.'

'Saying what?'

'I'm in control…you can't push me around.'

'I can't make breakfast wearing stilettos and a sharp suit. I dress like every other mum…' she explained obstinately.

Rafe saw the precise moment when the meaning of what she'd said hit her. For a split second the depth of her anguish was there for him to see. He'd like to throttle Chloe and her celebrity boyfriend!

Biting viciously down on her trembling lower lip, Tess steeled herself to meet the pity in his eyes. 'Only, of course, I'm not.' She spoke with quiet composure.

'Tess…' Frustration was building steadily inside him. Why the hell didn't she let him hug her instead of sprouting as many prickles as a porcupine?

Tess shook her head in silent rejection of his empathy. If he was nice to her now she'd make a total fool of herself.

'Anyhow, this conversation is academic—it's too late now for a make-over,' she babbled nervously. 'You can't make a silk purse out of…leave my hair alone!' she cried, batting away his intrusive hand.

His objective achieved, Rafe thrust the scrunchy thing he'd slid from her thick hair into his pocket, and gave her an unrepentant grin. 'Good,' he said, regarding his handi-work. 'But this…' with his other hand he began to tease out the ruthlessly restrained locks into a mass of gleaming soft waves '…is better…much better.'

'Now look what you've done!' Tess fumed, belatedly pulling away. She couldn't understand why she'd just stood there and let him. It wasn't as if she'd *enjoyed* the soft touch of his fingertips against her scalp. The drugged lethargy that had stolen over her couldn't possibly be classified along with pleasure.

'*I am.*' There was unnecessary force in his voice. There was also a weird expression on his face—it was the sort of expression that made Tess's heart thud and her throat close up.

'It's all mussed up.' She lifted a fretful hand to her head. 'I must look messy.'

'Want to muss mine?' he offered, raising a hand to his glossy raven head.

Hot desire smothered her like a heavy blanket. She couldn't breathe, she couldn't think—she could imagine, though. Her fingertips actually tingled as she imagined sinking them deep into that luscious dark mass to trace the outline of his skull.

Emerald eyes wide and shocked, she shook her head dumbly.

Rafe shrugged. 'Fair enough. Don't forget I offered, though.'

'I won't.'

'I think you should definitely aim for sexy, not neat.' His eyes were on the glossy waving chestnut strands that fell just below her shoulders. 'Competition will distract Chloe.'

That was uncalled for and a little bit cruel. 'Very funny!' she snapped. The day she could offer Chloe competition was never likely to dawn and they both knew it.

'If Chloe went out without her make-up and designer clothes nobody would give her a second glance.'

It occurred to Tess as he took hold of her chin and tilted her face first one way and then the other, subjecting her clear-cut profile to a comprehensive appraisal, that she really ought to complain about this sort of high-handed treatment.

'You've got the most incredible skin.' He made it sound like an accusation. 'All over,' he added hoarsely.

Tess stiffened and tugged her chin free. 'How would you

know?' Galloping alarm deepened the green of her eyes by several shades.

Rafe shrugged. 'I did put you to bed, and you weren't wearing anything under that...' he searched for an accurate description of her nightwear '...thing.'

'What a complete sleaze you are!' She choked, going hot and sweaty all over.

'My hand quite unintentionally—yes, *unintentionally*,' he repeated firmly in response to her hoarse derisive hoot, 'came into contact with your behind—*so hang me*! I could have dropped you—would you have preferred that? I'll remember the next time.'

'There won't be a next time.' Tess's breathing was laboured and noisy. She couldn't wipe away the image in her head of his fingers moving over... Self-derision swelled in her tight chest. Has it come to the point when sexual thrills are so sparse in my life that I'm reduced to wishing I'd been conscious while I was being accidentally groped?

'I had no idea you were such a prude.'

If he had been privy to some of the fantasies swirling around in her head, he'd know how wildly inappropriate that description was! 'Don't you dare take that patronising tone with me, Rafe Farrar!'

'And considering you were the one squirming and strangling me... Talk about overreaction.' He began to talk fast to cover up the fact that he'd just revealed how memorable her sleepy embrace was turning out to be. 'What did you think I'd done? I like a bit of response from the women I sleep with,' he teased.

'*Ben!*' Tess protested, her eyes belatedly going to the child who was happily immersing a toy car in the congealing remains of his cooked breakfast.

'Is not interested in what we're saying, and if I lower my voice much more I'll be whispering. I'll tell you something for nothing...'

Tess planted her hands on her slim hips and tossed her head. 'Since when was anything you said worth more?'

'You know,' he observed, eyeing her through narrowed, unfriendly eyes, 'you never used to be such an uptight bundle of repressions. Sex with me last night would have done you more good than half a bottle of vintage elderberry wine! For that matter,' he added grimly, 'it would have done me more good too.' If she tried to deny it he could always provide the proof...somehow he didn't think he'd find the task too tedious.

Total mind-blowing shock swept over Tess. She focused hard on the shock and outrage and turned a deaf ear to the pulsing excitement that all but deafened her.

'Have sex...with you!' she yelped, abandoning the hushed undertone they'd automatically adopted during their heated interchange in favour of strangled squeak.

'You make it sound as if the thought had never occurred to you!'

'It hasn't!' she responded, horrified.

'Like hell!' he thundered scornfully. 'You know perfectly well we've both been tiptoeing around it all morning.'

It was at this point Tess stopped pretending there was anything controlled about her panic. 'And I suppose you're going to tell me now what a great lover you are,' she sneered.

His eyes narrowed as he sucked in his breath sharply. 'Modesty forbids,' he drawled, 'but I can guarantee you wouldn't be this uptight this morning if we had had sex last night, and I might have actually got some sleep!'

'You think it would have been that boring...' She nodded and gave a twisted smile. 'You're probably right. I may have been happy playing the surrogate sister for you when we were kids but I'm not about to play the surrogate lover now!'

The idea of him closing his eyes and pretending she was the woman he loved filled her with an intense repugnance.

'I'm sure there are less…less *drastic* cures for insomnia,' she choked.

'A pill isn't going to solve my problem. Or yours.'

'And…' she cast a worried look in Ben's direction and lowered her voice to a hushed whisper '…sex is…?'

'No,' he conceded through gritted teeth, 'but it might make us both forget for a little while.'

The bleakness in his deep voice penetrated her anger and inconveniently touched her soft heart. She'd been too wrapped up in her own problems to think much about his.

'Is it really that bad for you, Rafe?' she asked sadly. Without being aware of what she was doing, she reached out and touched his face.

Eyes dark as night moved from the compassion shining in her eyes to her slim arm. His own hand came up to cover hers where it lay. She felt the controlled strength in the grip of his long fingers and shivered.

'Bad enough for me to think about sleeping with you, Tess?' He gave a harsh laugh. 'You really do take this modesty thing way too far. You're a lovely woman.'

'Not beautiful?' She didn't lay awake at night contemplating cosmetic surgery to correct her deficiencies, but right now making a joke about it was surprisingly hard.

'Beauty fades. You've got good bones,' he announced firmly.

'How poetic!'

'One of these days you're going to make one wisecrack too many,' he predicted darkly. 'As I was saying, when a man's in bed with an attractive woman his mind naturally turns to…' At least that was the way he'd eventually justified his fantasies during the long, *long* night.

'The gutter?' Maybe she was just starved for admiration of the male variety. It might explain the way her senses leapt in response to his casual announcement. After all, she knew it was just talk. If there had been any spark between them she'd have noticed years ago…it wasn't as if they hadn't had plenty of opportunities to have sex over the years if they'd wanted. They just hadn't wanted to.

'Is it so bad, Tess, to want to give and receive a little comfort?' The cynicism she hated was absent from his voice as his eyes slowly searched her face.

Put it like that and I sound churlish if I disagree. My God, but this man had a great way with words. It wasn't just what he said, it was the way he did it. Those eyes, that charisma—was it any wonder her brain had stopped functioning?

'No...yes...You're confusing me...' she protested weakly.

'The more I think about it, the more I think that closing the bedroom door and saying to hell with the world would be the best thing for us both!' He sank his fingers into the rich softness of her hair and brought his face down to hers. 'Who would we be hurting?' he growled.

Tess was sure there were several good answers to that husky, intimate question, but at that moment she couldn't bring one to mind.

'Right now you're hurting me.' She twisted her confined head a little to show him how. An ambiguous mixture of fear and excitement ripped through her as his fingers slid under the heavy weight of her hair down to the back of her neck.

The touch was like neat electricity; it blitzed along her nerve-endings. Eyes half closed, breath coming fast and shallow, Tess moved her head from side to side, not actually to resist the fresh constraint, more to appreciate the texture of his fingertips against her skin. Did it make her a sad, undersexed excuse for a woman that this was the single most sensual incident in her life?

Rafe felt the voluptuous shudder of pleasure that quivered through her slight frame and his eyes darkened. 'I knew you'd agree.' The intensity of his own relief took him by surprise. It was almost as great as the anticipation that sharpened every sense in his body.

Roused by the 'I told you so' note in his voice, Tess opened her mouth to put him right. She would have, too, in no uncertain terms if he hadn't at that same moment covered it with his.

Her eyes widened in shock and refocused on his face so close to her own. At this distance she could have appreciated how fine-textured his olive-toned skin actually was if she'd been in a fit state to think about such matters. It was the expression in his spectacular eyes, which like her own were open, that obliterated every other thought. She gave a deep sigh as her eyelids drooped over her burning eyes. The flood of pleasure was so intense, she moaned low in her throat, the sound merging with the masculine groan that vibrated deep in Rafe's chest.

Tess's hands clutched at empty space, and curled into tight balls to stop herself grabbing at him and hauling him on top of her... Yes, she realised as he lifted his head, that was *exactly* what she wanted to do.

Eyes spitting green flames, she wiped the back of her hand firmly across her mouth. It didn't stop her tasting him but she wasn't about to tell him that.

'You kissed me.'

'I'd have been disappointed if you hadn't noticed. What's the verdict?'

'The verdict is you're off your head if you think I'd agree to have sex with you!' She decided last minute to rephrase the *why would I do that*? She'd be deep in trouble if he took it into his head to show her why! 'If you can't read my body language, read my lips.' She pointed to her mouth and very slowly mouthed, 'Last night was the last time you'll be sharing my bed!'

CHAPTER FOUR

'THAT'S the sort of statement that is destined to come back and haunt you,' Rafe remonstrated, testing the springy resilience of the pouting curve of her lower lip with the tip of his thumb.

It was stupid to just stand there and let him take liberties, but for some reason Tess found she couldn't move. She was intensely conscious of the heavy aching feeling low in her belly.

'Just think how silly you're going to feel, angel, when I remind you of that the next time we're in bed together.'

Joke or no joke, his arrogance took her breath away. It did other things too, things like making her breasts tingle and swell against the thin top she wore. Graphic images crowded into her head, several involving sweaty bodies entwined. Her body temperature soared.

Tess caught her breath sharply and willed her weak limbs not to tremble. Angrily she wrenched her eyes away from the hypnotic warmth of his. She'd never expected to see the famed Farrar charisma this close up and she didn't imagine for one moment that it was accidental.

Even if he wasn't accustomed to rejection, it wasn't fair of him to use Tess to massage his damaged ego! Resentment mingled with a nerve-stretching excitement that made her head spin.

Serve him right if I bit him, she decided with uncharacteristic venom as her eyes continued to be mesmerised by the hand which probed the soft moisture of her inner lip.

She'd never before appreciated just how beautiful his elegant hands were, strong with the most lovely long, tapering fingers. Disturbingly, as her violent feeling evaporated, she was left with a compulsion to extend her tongue and run it… A tiny fearful moan escaped her parted lips… Cut this out, Tess! Right now.

She jerked her head away to dislodge his hand. His fingers trailed along the skin of her neck before they fell away completely. Tess gave a sigh of relief.

'One rejection and you've got to prove you've still got what it takes…?' she taunted hoarsely.

'And have I?'

She couldn't think of an honest reply that wouldn't seriously incriminate her.

The sound of distant voices became clearer. 'Here, have your keys! I'm sure I don't *want* to drive your beloved car again. It's not my fault the lane is so narrow. Aunty Tess!'

Tess fought her way through the fog of sexual arousal. It was like swimming against a particularly strong tide and several unfriendly currents.

Chloe! How the hell did I forget about her…? The answer was standing, all six feet four of him, beside her looking quite unfazed by the entrance of her two visitors.

'Trouble in Paradise?' Rafe wasn't looking at her guests when he spoke. Tess tore her eyes away from his mocking face and turned to face the music and her niece. Incredulity and shock warred for supremacy on her lovely young face as Chloe looked from her aunt to Rafe and back again. She didn't seem to like what she was seeing or thinking. Her full lips trembled.

Surely fuller than the last time Tess had seen them; the fleeting thought was replaced by far more urgent matters. Had Chloe seen and understood what was going on? Perhaps I should get her to explain it to me. Tess pushed aside this whimsical thought.

'Is that your car out there?' The surprisingly boyish face of Chloe's companion bore an apologetic grimace.

Rafe looked from the keys the older man was pocketing to Chloe. 'How bad is it?' he enquired stoically.

'Pooh! It's only a scratch!' Chloe protested dismissively.

Whatever Chloe had seen or understood about the scene she'd walked in on, it had made her look as sick as the proverbial parrot. Chloe might be in love with the handsome man beside her, who was, Tess noted worriedly, *much* older than he appeared on the small screen, but she obviously hadn't reached the point in her life where she could laugh at her teenage crush on Rafe.

A laugh—surely hysteria, for there was nothing *remotely* funny about this situation—was ruthlessly bitten back. Tess closed her eyes for a brief moment and forced her stiff lips into a welcoming smile.

'Chloe, how lovely to see you.' The patent insincerity jarred on her ears. 'And you must be Ian.'

It was at this point it struck home that during their altercation Rafe had taken hold of her wrist, which he now twisted neatly behind her back before plastering himself in a very misleading manner to her side.

Normally Tess wouldn't have thought twice about the casually affectionate body contact. Only normally Rafe hadn't just... What the hell had he just done—made a pass...? She didn't know and, she told herself firmly, she didn't much care. It was perfectly understandable for her to feel ultra-conscious and uncomfortable about the hardness of the muscular thigh that was tightly pressed against her. Struggling would make this all look worse than it already did.

The smile she received from the older man in return for her cautious one was warm and open. She'd expected to automatically feel antagonistic, only she didn't. She'd expected to get slick and instead she got sincere—it was pretty disorientating. Rafe had to take his share of the blame for her disorientation; the faint scent that rose from his body made her sensitive nostrils flare. It was so...so *male*.

'Ben, look who's here, it's Mummy.' Tess didn't see the startled expression on Rafe's face when she made the introductions.

The rigid smile was still fixed on her lips as she shot him a seething glare. It was hard to see the expression in his eyes from under the decadent sweep of his dark lashes. Her glance slid downwards to his mouth...don't think kissing...don't think kissing... Just what was he playing at now?

Ben didn't appear overly impressed by all the 'darlings', 'dear little Benjys' and 'isn't he sweet?' and even less impressed by the burning kisses pressed to his small grubby face. Tess dreaded what he might do any moment—when it came to tactlessness eighteen-month-olds were in class of their own. Ben might be limited verbally, but he had effective ways of making his likes and dislikes known!

Chloe smiled expectantly at Ben, who was not looking happy. Tess started to gush, she knew it, she could hear herself, but for the life of her she couldn't stop.

'He was so excited when I told him about your visit, he couldn't go to sleep last night. To make matters worse he was awake very early this morning. He's exhausted, but will he admit it? You know how it is with kids.' That's the problem, idiot, she reminded herself: Chloe doesn't begin to know how it is with kids, and certainly not this particular kid.

Would she know you had to look inside his wardrobe to check for aliens before he could go to sleep? Would she know he came out in a rash if he ate cheese, or that he threw up if he got too excited? The resentful pain inside was almost impossible to contain.

'It always makes him a little bit cranky if his routine is disrupted.'

'Are you calling me a disruption?' Rafe drawled.

Now that he mentioned it. Actually, Tess didn't mind the interruption, without which she might still be burbling on this time next week!

'She's called me worse,' he confided to his attentive audience.

'We wondered who belonged to the car outside.'

If Chloe's sharp blue gaze had missed a single detail of the tall, spectacular man's appearance the first time she'd subjected him to a slow head-to-toe scrutiny, she would have surely discovered it on the repeat performance.

Tess found herself feeling uncomfortable on Ian's behalf. A quick glance in his direction revealed he wasn't looking at Chloe, but at herself. She smiled tentatively back, relieved he was taking his fiancée's admiration of a much younger man so well.

'You look marvellous.'

Tess considered this observation a little unnecessary after all that drooling.

'Whatever brings you here of all places?' Chloe persisted, placing her hands on his shoulders and kissing the air artistically either side of his face.

Perhaps, Tess brooded, the stubble put her off. It wouldn't me... Rafe's eyes met hers over Chloe's head and she blushed, as any girl would caught looking at a man as if he were a piece of cream cake she couldn't wait to jam into her mouth.

'I always was eccentric.' Chloe didn't pick up on the irony in his voice—he hadn't expected her to—but rather to his surprise there was no answering gleam of humour in Tess's eyes either when he sought her gaze. 'It is my home, Chloe.'

'Oh, I expect you've come to see your grandfather.' Chloe looked happier now she'd come up with a reasonable explanation for finding him in her aunt's company. 'He's not dead, is he?' she enquired, with a worried afterthought. 'Silly me, of course he isn't. I mean, he's famous, isn't he? It would have been on the news.'

Rafe struggled to keep his face straight.

'I did come to see Grandfather,' he agreed. 'I arrived last night, actually, only I haven't made it out there yet.' He solicitously pounded Tess on the back as she began to choke.

Tess, her eyes still watering, watched the smile fade from Chloe's lips. She shot Tess a poisonous look before linking her arm through her partner's and pulling him forward. 'This is Ian!' she announced with a verbal flourish.

Shall I curtsy or just applaud? Tess wondered. It was obvious to her now why Ian hadn't been troubled by Chloe's interest in Rafe; the girl quite obviously worshipped him! Being worshipped must give a person a nice feeling of security, she mused wistfully.

'No need for introductions, Chloe, I know who Ian is. I never miss an episode.'

It was impossible to tell from the older man's polite expression if he believed Rafe's outright and not very convincing lie, and from the slight wince Tess detected as they exchanged a manly handshake she suspected it might have been firmer than was strictly required on Rafe's side. The urge to kick him intensified. What made him think she needed him to fight her battles for her?

Ian, who had up to this point reserved his attention for Tess, turned to the young woman who proudly wore his ring upon her finger. 'You didn't tell me you knew Rafe Farrar, darling. I'm surprised we've never met before, Rafe.'

'Yes, it's amazing,' Tess agreed, casting a malicious glance towards Rafe. 'Considering how Rafe hovers diligently around on the *lovey* fringes hoping someone will mistake him for someone *really* famous and take his photo.'

Tess was immediately mortified that she'd allowed Rafe to provoke her into this display of shrewish bad manners.

Ian's understanding expression reminded Tess that everything she knew about this man had been gleaned secondhand from Chloe. Given this fact, something might well have got lost in the translation! Tess had taken it for granted Chloe's love interest had an outsized ego and she'd hoped he had a mouse-sized intellect to match! Now it looked as if she was wrong on both counts.

'I hope Ben isn't too tired after his early start to come out with us for the day. We've got a picnic...'

'I ordered it from Fortnum's,' Chloe explained. Did she expect an eighteen-month-old to be impressed? Tess wondered.

'He loves the animals. Don't you, Ben...?' If the high-class hamper didn't include crisps and his favourite tuna-paste sandwiches Tess could foresee some toddler-sized tantrums on the horizon. If I was a nice person I'd warn them, she thought guiltily. Admit it, Tess, you're hoping exposure to a couple of Ben's best tantrums will make Chloe think twice about the joys of motherhood.

'He likes snakes best,' she elaborated. 'Hsss!' She demonstrated her best snake noise and Chloe looked at her as if she'd gone mad.

'Hsss, hsss,' Ben responded, displaying an immediate grasp of the situation.

'Then we'll definitely find some snakes for him.' Ian laughed.

Chloe looked almost comically horrified by her fiancé's easygoing response. Tess was glad about this for Ben's sake, of course she was, but at the same time she couldn't help thinking that the fact that he seemed a nice guy who didn't think kids came from another planet was not going to help her own case.

With Ian to support Chloe, the scene in which a tearfully grateful Chloe said, 'Ben belongs with you, Tess,' was growing fuzzier by the second.

'Don't you like nice furry things like...like...?' Chloe persisted hopefully.

'Rabbits?' Rafe put in helpfully. This was better than TV. If he hadn't been aware of how much Tess was suffering he'd have settled back to enjoy the entertainment.

Chloe smiled gratefully at him. 'Yes, bunnies. Do you like sweet little bunnies, Benjy?'

'Hsss.' Ben chortled happily.

'Would everyone like coffee?' Tess leapt in to fill the silence that followed and took the opportunity to remove herself as far from Rafe as possible.

'Very kind, but we ought to be off. We'll have him back in time for tea.'

'Ess,' Ben appealed, holding out his arms to Tess.

Tess ached to pick him up. 'Not today, Ben.'

'Some other time, perhaps,' Ian agreed. 'It's been nice to meet you, Tess. I hope you won't mind if I don't call you aunt.'

'Almost anything else would be preferable,' Tess admitted bluntly.

'You're not at all what I was expecting…' A faint twitch of Ian's photogenic lips accompanied this last wry comment.

Despite the bleakness that had settled around her heart, Tess responded with wry humour. 'Let me guess—a shawl, slippers and rheumatism?'

'Well, not Titian hair and great bones, at any rate.' He studied her face with the objective eye of a connoisseur.

The *objectivity* didn't fool Rafe for one second!

'The camera would just love that face, it's so expressive.' Rafe rolled his eyes.

Tess, who was trying hard not to be expressive, looked uncomfortable.

'Have you ever done any acting or—?'

Tess, aware that her niece was looking ready to pull out the said Titian hair follicle by follicle, cut him off hastily. 'I don't have my Equity card, and isn't there a bit more to being an actor than a pretty face?'

'Tess, you really haven't watched my programme, have you?' he chided her with attractive self-derision. 'Still, at least nobody has ever accused me of being highbrow and élitist.'

Tess found it hard not to laugh as she listened to this sly jibe. Ian might not be accusing Rafe directly, but he didn't really have to—a high-profile victim of Rafe's lethal interviewing techniques had recently made both accusations loudly on national television.

'Well, shouldn't you do something with his face and hands before we take him?' Chloe, toe tapping impatiently, looked pointedly at Ben's grubby hands.

'You're right, Chloe.' Tess subdued her natural instincts to respond to the child's need and held her ground. If Chloe wanted to be a mum, fine, she could be a mum and all that entailed. The sooner she learnt there was more to the job than supplying presents and picnic hampers, the better. 'You know where the bathroom is, there's a pile of fresh nappies in the wicker basket, and I left a change of clothes out in his bedroom.'

'Nappies?' Chloe echoed, looking pale.

If Ian was worrying about sticky baby fingers on his upholstery, he didn't show it. Tess wished she could figure out what the expression on his face meant as he watched Chloe, wearing her plucky but ill-used heroine face, leave the room with her son.

'I think I'd better give her a hand,' he said, excusing himself after a moment with an attractive smile.

He might not be as tall or as young as he appeared on the screen, but he was a million times warmer and more human.

'He's nice, isn't he?' As stepfather material went, they probably didn't get much better, Tess admitted gloomily to herself. The male influence was something she had never been able to supply in Ben's life and, things being the way they were, probably never would.

'*Nice!*' Rafe's tongue curled around the word with scathing distaste.

His vicious tone startled Tess, who twirled around to face him.

'Do you mean you actually swallowed all that Titian hair, great bones, I'll get you a screen test guff?' His laughter was nothing short of insulting. 'Besides,' he added in a disgruntled tone, 'you don't have *Titian* hair.' His brooding glance strayed and paused on the top of her shining head 'It's chestnut.'

'Just like your dumpy old pony eating her head off in your grandfather's stables,' she suggested with a spurt of childish petulance. Titian might not be strictly accurate, but it had a much more glamorous sound to it than chestnut

'Much glossier, actually.' Rafe had the strongest urge to let the glossy strands run through his fingers. He actually started to reach out before it occurred to him that this might not be the moment for spontaneous tactile gestures. 'Talk about laying it on with a trowel! I didn't think you were that simple, Tess! The man's a complete con artist.'

'Meaning he's automatically insincere if he thinks I'm good to look at.' A dangerous note crept into her voice as she lifted her arms from her sides and subjected her jeans-clad figure to a tight-lipped critical scrutiny. 'You're just mad because he got your measure at first glance.'

'I *mean*,' Rafe corrected impatiently, 'that the man knows you could make things difficult for them. He's trying to keep you sweet. No, cancel that, he's *succeeding* in keeping you sweet, though if he carries on being so full-on playing up to you,' he predicted with grim satisfaction, 'he's going to have trouble on his hands with Chloe. She looked fairly green, and I can't say I blame her!'

'You don't blame her!' Tess echoed incredulously. 'I don't believe you, I really don't. Ian is right, you have become an intellectual snob,' she breathed wrathfully, shaking her head slowly from side to side. 'Unusual it may be, but I'm not so *desperate* yet that I turn into some sort of compliant puppet when a man says something flattering to me. I was simply making an objective observation.'

'Objective, *sure*!'

'Well, a damned sight more objective than you're being. What are you frowning like that for?' she snapped.

'I was trying to figure out how come you called Chloe *Mummy* in front of Ben?'

'Because she is!' Tess wondered if he was being dense just to annoy her. 'That's no secret.'

'Pardon me, but I thought it was?' Rafe began with a frown. 'You mean he…Ben…knows?' he puzzled.

'Of course he knows. Well,' she modified, 'he knows, but he only understands as much as any one-year-old can under the circumstances. I may wish I was Ben's mother but I know I'm not,' she told him fiercely. 'And I'm neither stupid or selfish enough to lie to him. People assume I'm Ben's mum and I don't go out of my way to explain the relationship, but if they ask me…'

'You mean if *I'd* asked…?'

'I'd have told you, sure I would. Only you didn't ask. In fact, you didn't say much at all, the way I recall it.' It was the one time she could recall when Rafe had genuinely been at a loss for words.

'Well, what did you expect?' he exploded.

Tess pressed an urgent finger to her lips and glanced furtively up the stairs. 'Will you keep your voice down?' she hissed nervously.

'If you want to whisper in your own house that's up to you, but I'm damned if I will!'

'That would only make any sort of sense if this was your house and, even though you treat it as if it is, it isn't! Which makes that an extremely silly thing to say.'

'Your house, my house!' He clicked his fingers dismissively. 'The point is you hadn't even told me you were pregnant! That tends to make a bloke who was supposedly your best friend feel excluded.'

Tess's lips twitched. 'I probably didn't tell you because I wasn't pregnant,' she reminded him. 'It's not my fault that you turned out to be judgemental and narrow-minded,' she announced with sweet malice.

The breath hissed out from between his clamped teeth. 'I like that!' He didn't sound or look as if he liked anything she was saying. 'I tried to be supportive, it was you who gave me the cold shoulder. You used that patronising little smile to make me feel male and useless, then for good measure retreated behind that bottle of formula!' he accused.

'You *are* male and useless.'

'You've not got that bottle of formula to hide behind.'

Tess's chin went up. 'Is that a threat?' She was horrified to hear that give-away catch in her husky voice. It was the sort of catch that turned a question into an invitation. There was no escaping the fact that *breathless* was entirely the wrong message to be sending!

'It's a simple observation.'

Tess didn't find anything simple about the dangerous gleam in his dark eyes. 'Well, you can keep your observations to yourself,' she blustered. 'And that goes for your hands too,' she added for good measure. 'I don't know what you were playing at...'

'You know, I always wondered why you didn't breast-feed.' His eyes rested thoughtfully on the area involved. It took all of her will-power not to cover herself with her hands. She didn't dare look down; it was bad enough just *feeling* what effect his scrutiny was having.

She forced herself to breathe. 'Well, now you know.'

'Now I know.'

Tess silently prayed his knowledge didn't extend to the state of her rioting hormones.

'Chloe's wondering whether we're sleeping together.'

His expression suggested this was a good thing and she should congratulate him... She should probably strangle him. A fleeting glance at the strong brown column of his neck made her wonder what it would feel like to run her fingers... Her homicidal urges were replaced by other far more disturbing urges.

'*I wonder why?*' Tess drawled hoarsely.

'I think it's probably better for you to worry about what I'm going to do or say than worry about losing Ben. When you saw their car pull up you looked frantic.'

The provocation of his cool words made Tess abandon her discreet whisper. 'Your groping might have been purely altruistic, but it felt like groping to me!' she yelled.

'I didn't say that. The distraction part was good but I groped you...I prefer fondled,' he mused. 'It has a much nicer sound to it. I fondled you because I can't do what I actually want to.' The mocking smile faded totally from his face. 'Aren't you going to ask me what that is?'

'No...no!' she denied, shaking her head vigorously from side to side. 'Now will you just shut up?' she snapped, hearing the clatter of feet on the staircase. 'They're coming.'

This time he would be coming home, she thought as she watched Ben being strapped into the car; the next time she could be waving farewell for good. Contemplating this event was so painful that Tess made her excuses and dashed back into the house before the car had drawn away. She'd only just reached the kitchen when Chloe's breathless return to the kitchen ruined her bitter introspection.

'I forgot my bag...see,' Chloe explained, producing a decorative sugar-pink number that wasn't big enough to hold a comb.

Her next words were so calculated to injure—and injure they did—that Tess no longer had any doubts that the bag had been deliberately left behind.

'I'm not heartless. I know how you must feel losing Benjy. But I'm his mother.' She sighed. 'One day when you have a child of your own...' Her hand went to her mouth. 'Sorry, Tess, I forgot—you can't, can you?'

'No, I can't.'

Something that might have been remorse flickered in Chloe's blue eyes before she remembered how Tess had shamelessly monopolised the male attention.

'Does Rafe know?'

'Know what?'

'That you can't have a baby of your own.'

'There's no reason he should know,' Tess replied, won

dering when Chloe would decide she'd sunk her knife in deep enough.

'Then you're not sleeping with him...?'

Tess didn't feel inclined to make Chloe feel any happier so she avoided giving a direct answer. 'I don't give my medical history to all my lovers,' she replied, fighting hard to retain her fragile composure.

'A word to the wise, Tess. I thought Rafe looked a bit embarrassed when you were throwing yourself at him earlier. I'm only telling you this—'

'I know,' Tess interrupted drily. 'Out of the goodness of your heart. Your concern is noted, but actually, Chloe, I'm not sure the situation has been invented which could embarrass Rafe.' Irritate, annoy and aggravate, yes; embarrass, no!

'You know me so well.' Despite the laconic drawl, Rafe was showing classic signs of annoyance at that moment.

'Rafe!' The voice at her shoulder made Chloe spin around. Her much practised flirtatious smile faded as she absorbed the furious contempt in his eyes. 'I didn't see you there.'

'I know, and just for the record, Chloe, your aunt isn't a kiss-and-tell sort of lady.' Rafe didn't spare her more than a few seconds before he turned his attention to Tess, but the contact had been long enough for Chloe to feel as bad about herself as she ever had allowed herself to.

'I'll be off, then,' Chloe said weakly.

'Might be a good idea,' Tess agreed without looking at her niece.

'Is it true?' Rafe stepped over the threshold and closed the door firmly behind him.

Tess's unrealistic hope that he hadn't been standing there long enough to hear what Chloe had said vanished.

'I thought you'd gone.' She picked up a plate from the table and promptly dropped it on the floor where it smashed into a thousand pieces. 'Look what you made me do...' Her voice quivered.

'I asked you a question.'

'I chose not to answer it,' she responded flippantly.

'Will you stop doing that? You're going to cut yourself.' He came up behind her and, arms around her narrow ribcage, hauled her to her feet. He brushed the tiny fragments of powdery china off her knees before straightening up himself. Placing his fingers beneath her chin, he searched with grim eyes the flushed face she turned reluctantly up to him.

'I wish you wouldn't tower over me.'

'Blame my genes and a well-balanced diet.'

'Let go of me,' she whispered shakily.

'You can't have children...?'

Tess closed her eyes. 'That's right, I'm sterile.'

Or as good as damn it, anyhow! Improbable, but not impossible was the way the doctor who had patiently explained about her condition had put it. He'd gone on to speak at length about IVF and associated treatments, but Tess, who irrationally had felt as if her very femininity had been cast into doubt by the news, hadn't actually taken in much of what he'd said.

She supposed that it was something she'd just taken for granted...the fact that one day she'd meet someone and they'd have children. She had never actually thought about it and if anyone had asked her she wouldn't have claimed to be a particularly maternal person. It was only when she'd realised this was never going to happen that she'd known how strong the desire to one day be a mother was.

'You didn't tell me.'

This resentful observation wrenched a bitter laugh from her. 'It isn't the sort of thing that crops up in conversation very often! By the way, when my appendix burst that time it seems it left me a bit tied up, quite literally.'

Rafe winced. He couldn't begin to imagine what this sort

of thing meant to a woman. 'How long have you known about it?'

'About five years.'

The sound of his startled inhalation was audible. 'So long…?' he wondered.

'And, no matter what Chloe implied, it wouldn't make any difference if I could have a hundred children of my own—no child could replace Ben!' She glared at him obstinately, daring him to think otherwise.

He swore. 'I know that, Tess.'

She glared but his dark eyes were kind and caring. Tess felt her antagonism slide away, leaving a raw sadness in its place.

'I know you know,' she mumbled indistinctly as with a sigh she finally allowed herself to relax into the embrace and succour his waiting arms offered.

'You should have told me.'

'I wish I had,' she mumbled honestly. Deep down she supposed she'd been afraid that Rafe would look at her differently when he knew.

She didn't weep, she just held onto him as though her life depended on it. In his turn Rafe stroked her hair, caressed the curve of her spine. It wasn't the soft, silly things he said that comforted her so much as the reassuring sound of his deep voice.

'Thanks.' Feeling suddenly intensely shy, Tess experienced an urgent desire to be released from the strong arms that held her. Rafe seemed to have no trouble interpreting the sudden rigidity in her slender body.

Standing back on her own two feet, she smoothed her hair and avoided his compassionate eyes.

'You know, maybe it would be better if Chloe does have Ben to live with her and Ian,' she announced, trying to look at the problem objectively. 'I've never been able to offer Ben a father. A boy needs a man in his life…role model…that sort of thing…'

'You'll marry one day and someone who'd be a better role model than that creep Chloe's got herself involved with.'

Given Rafe's antagonism to Ian, Tess decided to leave the *creep* issue well alone. She shook her head firmly. 'No, I'll never get married.'

'You say that now, but when you meet someone...'

It made Tess angry that he was just telling her what he thought she wanted to hear—a pretty pointless exercise when they both knew the reality was that no man would want her once he knew the truth.

'I said *never.*' Her expression hardened. 'Marriage is all about providing a loving, secure environment for children. That's why a man gets married.'

'That's why women get married,' he corrected. 'They're the practical ones. A man gets married for other reasons.'

'You really don't have to try and make me feel better, Rafe. I've had a lot of time to get used to the idea and I'm quite realistic about it.'

'That must account for the saintly aura,' he snapped. 'Who made you the expert on what men want?'

His anger continued to confuse her. 'Well, I'm not, but—'

'But nothing! I can see that you've written yourself this naff script that says you've got to be brave and stoical, and quite frankly it makes me want to wring your stupid neck.'

'I'd noticed,' she responded faintly.

'Being a man.'

'I'd noticed that too.' On reflection this was a subject it might be better not to pursue.

'I feel,' he continued, in no mood to be sidetracked by her interruptions, 'that I'm *slightly* better qualified to comment on the subject than you. We get some bad press but most men are thinking about love when they get married, Tess, not good child-bearing hips...' His eyes slid of their own volition to a point below Tess's tiny waist. He cleared his throat; it wasn't the child-bearing qualities or lack of them that made it hard for him to look away.

'You're talking about sex. A man doesn't have to get married to have sex, Rafe. But then I'm not telling you something you didn't already know, am I?'

'There's a difference between sex and love, one which even we *shallow* men can recognise.'

Tess blinked at the angry intensity of his words. Oh, God, she'd forgotten; he'd loved and lost! It was small wonder that under the circumstances he felt passionate about the subject.

'Is that why you wanted to get married, Rafe?'

With a frown he brushed aside her slightly wistful question. 'We're not discussing me.'

'That fact seems rather unfair considering we're having an open day on my most intimate feelings,' she grumbled.

'One day I'm sure you'll find the man who wants you for you, not for what you can provide him with.'

'A nice thought...'

'You don't believe me, do you?'

She folded her arms across her chest and gave him a clear-eyed direct look. 'Frankly, no. When I told Andrew, he was off as fast as his four-by-four would take him.' She didn't add that that had been the desired outcome.

'You told the vet?' For some reason the fact that Tess had shared her secret with another man—especially *that* one— while he had been kept in the dark incensed Rafe.

'Well, he did propose to me.'

'Damn cheek!' Rafe muttered. 'All that goes to prove is what a prize pillock he is.'

This was going a bit far, considering Rafe had never spoken to Andrew above twice as far as she knew.

'What is it with you, Rafe?' she puzzled. 'Do you take a dislike to any man I like on principle? I thought women were meant to be the irrational ones.'

'Irrational! Me?' Rafe looked predictably amazed at the idea.

'First Andrew and now Ian. The poor man hasn't done anything but be pleasant.'

'The *poor* man is the pathetic type who at the first sign of a receding hairline and expanding waistline—'

'I didn't see either on Ian,' she couldn't resist interjecting.

'He spends a sack full of money to make sure you don't.'

'God, but you've got a cruel tongue.'

'Stock in trade, angel,' he admitted unrepentantly. 'Your Ian has nabbed himself the first nubile young beauty who is stupid, or infatuated enough—in Chloe's case both—to make himself an object of universal envy. His mates will pat him on the back and call him a hell of a bloke! It's classic.'

'It's a generalization, is what it is,' she retorted scornfully.

He tried another tack. 'Are you trying to tell me that you approve of an age gap that dramatic, Tess?'

'I can see it might be problematic,' Tess conceded, 'but it shouldn't matter when two people are in love.'

'I always knew you were a closet romantic under all that pragmatism.' Mockery glittered savagely in his dark eyes. 'At this point I'm resisting my natural inclination to quote Ben...' She looked back at him blankly. *'Mush?'* he reminded her.

'I don't blame you for being bitter...' She cleared her throat, skating delicately around his masculine sensitivity. 'It's only natural that you feel a little bit cynical at the moment.'

'I'm cynical for a living,' he snarled.

'There's no need to sound so proud of it,' she remonstrated tartly.

'I take it you fall into the love-conquers-all camp...with one significant exception.'

Confusion flickered across her face. 'What exception?'

'Yourself.'

The colour that had only recently returned to her cheeks rapidly receded. 'That's different.'

'Odd,' he drawled. 'I rather thought it would be.'

'And I wouldn't know, would I, never having been in love?'

He looked thunderstruck by her angry assertion. *'Never!'*

If he knew some of the other things she'd never done, he'd *really* stare! 'I've no desire to discuss my love life with you. Who asked for your opinion about anything anyhow?' Her face stiff with defensive disdain, she tossed her head, sending the warm rich strands of hair whipping across her face. 'For that matter, who asked you to stay?'

'Perhaps I find your *warmth* slightly less chilly than the reception I'll no doubt receive at home.'

His ironic twisted smile aggravated the hell out of her. It wouldn't have taken much effort to pretend the pleasure of her company had anything to do with it, but why be kind when you could be sarcastic? Wasn't that just Rafe all over?

'I don't know why you insist on fighting with your grand-father. He's an old man...'

Rafe's lips twitched. 'I'll tell him you said so. The news of his decrepitude should go down nearly as well as the knowledge his death should make it onto the six o'clock news. I thought maybe you could do with a friend around.' His broad shoulders lifted dismissively. 'It would seem I was wrong. I'll make myself scarce.' He bent to pick up the jacket he'd discarded over the back of a chair the previous evening.

CHAPTER FIVE

'YOU'RE going…?' Perversely the thought filled Tess with dismay. Why the panic? It's not as if I'm not used to being alone.

'Wasn't that the idea?'

'Yes…no…'

Rafe's dark brows drew into a quizzical line. 'Are you making me a better offer?' He'd intended the question to be ironic, then he saw the expression on her face and he grew very still.

Tess's eyes widened. Am I…? The muscles of her pale smooth throat worked as her lips moved silently. Why not? some inner reckless voice challenged. It's what you want isn't it…? It's what you haven't stopped thinking about.

'Well, Tess…?' he prompted with husky impatience.

'I don't think I want to be alone. I'll just be sitting here…thinking…' She swallowed. 'I want what's best for Ben, but I don't want to lose him.' She fought back a sob and caught the pink flesh of her lower lip between her teeth. 'Do you think I'm very selfish?' Her wide green eyes fixed on his face.

Rafe swallowed hard. 'No more than the rest of us. I'll stay if you want, Tess,' he agreed hoarsely and was rewarded with a watery smile. 'But you've got to promise me one thing.'

'What?'

'Don't look at me like that!' he pleaded throatily.

'I don't understand…'

'Men have hormones, Tess, and I'm no exception. Do you hear what I'm saying?'

She heard, all right. She raised her hand and touched the

79

side of his face. It wasn't an innocent action and she felt a surge of satisfaction when Rafe jerked away.

'I've got hormones too,' she whispered softly. 'And I've been thinking about what you said before…' It wasn't until the confession emerged that she realised just how much she'd been thinking about it.

'I say a lot of things,' he reflected grimly. 'Some more worth listening to than others.'

Was this his way of saying he hadn't really meant it…he'd just been talking big, safe in the knowledge that she'd never call his bluff? Only a total idiot could fail to recognise that this situation had a potential for humiliation on a big scale, and Tess was no idiot. But she found she'd gone too far to back down now. Besides, a compulsion she didn't recognise was driving her onwards.

'I want to…' Tess swallowed to relieve the aching constriction in her throat. Her eyes shone with unshed tears as she willed herself not to flinch from Rafe's gaze. 'I want to forget…I want to feel…' The words sounded so breathily *needy* that for a moment she couldn't believe they'd emerged from her own mouth.

He still hadn't said anything, which was definitely not a good sign. She wasn't sure whether it was obstinacy or lunacy that made her stumble on regardless.

'Don't look at me like that. You're the one who planted the idea in my head!' she shouted resentfully. '*You* said we wouldn't be hurting anyone. *You* said there was nothing wrong in giving and receiving a little comfort…' She tried not to think about how flawed she'd found his logic at the time.

Rafe didn't need reminding of what he'd said any more than he needed telling he couldn't go through with it if he had any shred of decency left.

'I could do with a little comfort right now.' Actually, she reflected, what I actually need is a great dollop of the stuff.

It was the harsh sound of Rafe's sharp inhalation that

finally brought her reckless babble to an abrupt halt. The enormity of what she'd done hit her with the force of a runaway truck.

She didn't—she *couldn't* look at him as she stumbled towards the door. 'Please, forget I said any of that, it was stupid, I didn't mean...' If only that were true, she would feel less cringeingly humiliated.

'Tess!'

She flinched away from the touch of his hand on her shoulders; the contact was like a jolt of neat electricity running through her body.

'Don't think I took any of that stuff you said this morning seriously.'

He couldn't let her walk away looking like that; perhaps she'd feel better if he confessed he didn't feel so crash-hot happy himself!

Rafe rapidly discovered that making Tess stop still long enough to listen to him—to look at him, even—wasn't as simple a task as he'd bargained for. She struggled against the light restraint as if her life depended on it. Rafe could hardly credit that anyone who appeared as physically delicate as Tess could be so strong. He was afraid she'd hurt herself, or him—the Marquess of Queensberry would have been shocked out of his wig by her tactics—before she exhausted herself.

'You've got a kick like a mule!' He winced as her foot made contact for the second time with his shin. 'You'll give up before I do...' he promised.

Tess gave up so abruptly she almost slithered out of his arms onto the floor. It took a couple of seconds for enough strength to return to her legs to enable them to take her weight and when it did she had only one thought in her head...*escape*!

Rafe's hands closed around her wrists as she began to back impetuously away from him. He could feel the resistance was purely superficial; her heart was no longer in it.

He let her struggle weakly for a moment before jerking her towards him.

'I'm sorry you don't believe I meant what I said,' he grated, speaking from between clenched teeth, 'because I meant every word of it. There's nothing I'd like better than to take you to bed, but you're...'

Was this patent untruth supposed to make her feel better? 'I'm what, Rafe?' She stood passively and turned a seething, resentful gaze upon him. 'Too thin, too ugly, too *easy*...?'

'A man doesn't take advantage when someone is hurting as much as you are. I mean, under normal circumstances would you want to sleep with me? Let alone ask—' He stopped abruptly.

'Don't be squeamish, Rafe, spit it out!' she recommended bitterly. 'We both know I asked you to take me to bed. Why,' she pondered aloud, 'I decide to change the habit of a lifetime and be spontaneous now, I've not the faintest idea.'

'Emotional trauma will do that to a person.'

'Let's leave my emotional trauma out of this for a second, shall we? I'm curious—what man doesn't take advantage? *You?*' Her voice rose to an incredulous squeak. 'You were perfectly willing to take advantage this morning,' she jeered.

A dull colour ran up under his tan. 'I wasn't thinking. I'd be using you!'

Thinking wasn't all it was cracked up to be. If he hadn't started now we'd be... It brought a hectic flush to her cheeks to think about where they'd be if she'd had her wanton way.

'Maybe I want to be used!'

'You don't mean that, Tess.'

'I hate it when you tell me what I mean!'

'I was being selfish, and right now,' he announced explosively, 'at this precise second I have an overwhelming urge to be *extremely* selfish.' The hunger in his restless glance was immensely soothing to Tess's bruised self-esteem—and injurious to her pulse-rate.

That *extremely* sounded very promising and there was no

mistaking the sincerity in his loaded announcement. Relief washed over her. It was slightly less humiliating if the person you'd thrown yourself at found you moderately attractive.

'You do...?' The line between her shapely eyebrows deepened suspiciously.

'Give a man a break, Tess. I'm trying to do the decent thing here, and...' his impressive chest heaved deeply '...if you must know, it's painful!'

'Good!' She meant it, and it showed.

A sliver of amusement slid across his sternly handsome face. 'I'm really glad my agony gives you pleasure. Seriously, Tess...'

'I never stopped being serious.'

'Sex is no cure-all when life stinks.'

She choked quietly on her disbelief. Talk about moving the goalposts! 'You've changed your tune.' For that matter, so have I!

'We're not talking about me, we're talking about you. You're not the type that goes in for casual sex,' he announced firmly.

He thought he would have noticed if Tess had had a string of lovers. Of course, there must have been some, but she'd been pretty discreet. The thought of these anonymous individuals didn't improve his humour.

Does he think I don't already know that? Knowing it hadn't stopped her throwing herself at him like some sex-starved bimbo.

'But you are?'

'No, of course not,' he denied with irritated impatience. 'I'm strictly into monogamy.'

'*Serial* monogamy.'

'If you like,' he conceded testily. 'I'm trying to explain that I can separate my emotions from—'

'Sex!' she supplied shrilly. 'Neat trick, Rafe,' she admired.

The nerve in his clenched jaw started jumping again. 'You only *think* you want to go to bed with me.'

'Now the man knows what I'm thinking! Is there no end to his talents?' she marvelled.

'I'm not going to be responsible for—'

'For what, exactly?' she interrupted hotly. 'This is sex we're talking here, not a lifelong commitment. You think you'd spoil me for other men? You think sleeping with you would be so great I'd fall instantly and inconveniently in love with you? My God, but you really do rate yourself highly these days.'

His sternly reproachful look silenced her scornful laughter. It made her feel mean and petty. What he said next intensified the feeling.

'We're mates...?'

Tess found herself nodding mutely in reply to the probing look in his dark eyes.

'I wouldn't want anything to spoil that, Tess. Not my libido or your loneliness...'

'How do you know I'm lonely?' Lonely had such a pathetic, loserish ring to it. Such an *accurate* ring to it, she acknowledged reluctantly. Without Ben her life was empty. She found herself wondering uncomfortably whether there wasn't some element missing even with Ben. 'As a matter of fact, I'm celibate out of choice, not necessity!'

Rafe thought he probably hid his surprise at this unsolicited piece of information quite well; he didn't have as much success keeping a lid on his raging curiosity.

'How long...?' The pink tinge of her skin became a deeper red as she glared back at him. He held up a pacifying hand. 'None of my business.'

'Too right it isn't,' she growled belligerently.

'I know Chloe's decision has turned your life upside down until you don't know day from night...'

Thoughtfully Tess nodded her head.

'Or friend from lover.'

He was talking sense, of course, but that didn't stop her stomach doing a double flip when she looked at his mouth. It was totally irrational, but she'd never craved anything in her life as much as she craved the touch of Rafe's lips against hers, the touch of his hands on her overheated skin. *Hell-fire, girl, it's your overheated imagination you need to worry about!*

'And Claudine has done much the same thing to me.'

Tess pushed aside the embarrassing problem of her sensual preoccupation. 'Claudine is the one...?'

His nostrils flared. 'Yes, she's the one.'

A sharp, sobering stab of jealousy lanced through her. 'I'm sorry, Rafe.' Her small hand closed over his forearm. *Some friend I am.* The warmth in her voice was to compensate for her shameful gut response. Tess's indignation rose. *What a bitch this woman must be! Just because Rafe came across as pretty invulnerable, there was no need to play fast and loose with his emotions.*

'I thought you prescribed a dose of humility.' He looked from the sincerity of her upturned face to the small hand on his sleeve.

'I'm a sanctimonious cow sometimes.'

Amused affection deepened the creases around his eyes. 'I don't think there's anything remotely bovine about you, Tess. Possibly something slightly feline,' he suggested, his mind flickering back to the way she'd wound herself around him as he'd carried her upstairs the previous night. She certainly had the suppleness of a cat and the green eyes. The smile faded from his own eyes.

Tess had always thought it a cruel twist of fate that a man could have ludicrously long, luscious eyelashes she would have given her eye-teeth for. Now she found herself wondering why she'd never noticed before how expressive those lash-shielded eyes were.

'You can tell me about it if you like,' she offered bravely.

Wasn't that what friends were for…listening? It was just tough that the subject happened to make her skin crawl.

'Who needs sex when you have good old-fashioned friendship?' Rafe wondered harshly. The skin was stretched tightly over the sharp planes and intriguing angles of his strong face. Tess watched dry-mouthed as his breathing perceptively quickened.

'Exactly. We won't even mention sex again,' she agreed miserably.

Her sensible smile faded and died as his hooded eyes continued to rest unblinkingly on her pale face. 'Forbidden subject…?'

Tess nodded. She couldn't take her eyes from the erratic pulse that beat beside his mouth. The silence stretched on and on almost to breaking-point.

'Tess…?' A fine sheen of moisture glistened on the bronzed skin of his face.

She could hardly make out the faraway sound of his curiously strained voice over the slow but thunderous pounding of her own heart.

'Yes, Rafe?'

'It's not important.' His eyes closed and his head went back, displaying the strong line of his throat. After a long tension-soaked moment he lifted it; his eyes were blazing with reckless purpose.

'Yes!' he yelled. 'Yes, it damn well is important! For pity's sake, woman! Kiss me!' he groaned thickly, lunging towards her.

With a small cry of relief Tess closed her arms tightly about his neck as he swung her up off the ground. She could feel the febrile tremors that ran through his lean body.

'Tess…Tess…Tess…' He interspersed the fevered kisses he rained over her face with husky repetitions of her name. 'I know this is slightly crazy, but, God help me,' he breathed against her ear, 'I've got to do this or I'll…'

She didn't want his apologies, she wanted his kisses. 'Me too,' she confessed ecstatically.

To the casual observer, the inarticulate but encouraging noises that emerged from her aching throat might have sounded like whimpers, but Rafe didn't seem to have any trouble interpreting them. He tightened his grip on Tess's pliant frame, drawing it closer to his body, which betrayed even more overtly than his lips did the driving urgency that held him in its grip.

The flurry of shock at discovering just how urgent Rafe was feeling dissipated as a flood of wild, sensual need washed over her. Tess's lips moved inexpertly but with boundless enthusiasm over the hard, clean-cut contours of his olive-skinned face, taking delight in the faintly salty taste of his flesh until their lips finally collided. The collision came not a moment too soon for her needs.

His teeth tugged at the soft, tender skin of her pink parted lips before, with a deep groan, his tongue plunged inside, plundering the moist, receptive warmth of her mouth. The shock of the contact slid so swiftly through her body, the fallout hit her toes even before she started kissing him back with a hunger and urgency that matched his.

Lips still attached to hers, Rafe cleared the table with a single sweeping gesture just before he sat her down on the hard surface.

'We'll still be friends...'

Tess curled her legs around his slim hips and continued to press her lips to the smooth, strong column of his neck while nodding her enthusiastic agreement to his defiant observation.

'That goes without saying.' She lifted her head and found his eyes had a hot, unfocused expression. On seeing that dark, dangerous look she felt a delicious shiver of anticipation join the tiny rivulets of sweat running down her quivering spine.

She let out an ecstatic cry and her body arched when his

hand brushed against the engorged peak of one aching breast.

'Hush,' he soothed thickly as she bit her lip. 'You're so wonderfully sensitive,' he marvelled, his eyes on the point where her nipples protruded through the cotton covering of her dark top. As her lips began to move Rafe bent his head to catch her faint words.

'If we were strangers I couldn't want you to do this.'

She insinuated her hand through the gap where two buttons on his shirt had parted company. Tess felt his powerful stomach muscles contract helplessly as she spread her fingers wide over his amazingly satiny skin. Rafe held her eyes as he hooked a finger under the top button of his shirt and pulled it down impatiently. Several buttons flung across the room as the fabric gaped open.

The breath caught in Tess's throat as her hot, slumberous gaze moved hungrily over his incredibly hard body. His skin glistened under its fine covering of sweat. There wasn't an ounce of surplus flesh to conceal the perfect muscle definition of his broad chest with its light sprinkling of dark hair and washboard-flat belly. Intermittent quivers ran visibly through his body, making the muscles just below the surface ripple. He was quite, *quite* perfect, she thought gloatingly.

'You're right, we don't need the dinner dates and the awkward pauses. We don't need to waste time on all those tedious preliminaries.' If she didn't agree he was in deep trouble! 'We already know everything there is to know about each other,' he panted, tugging her black tee shirt free of the waistband of her jeans and pushing his hands under the thin cotton. Her warm skin felt unbelievably smooth under his hands.

Tess's heavy eyelids lifted to reveal a sultry stare. 'Not quite *everything*, but hopefully we will before much longer.' Her wicked throaty chuckle delighted him before it was lost inside the warmth of his mouth.

The big, strong hand that touched the side of her face wasn't quite steady. 'It's a natural progression.'

Was he trying to convince himself? She didn't waste more than a second on that thought because she was just as eager as he was to skip the preliminaries and satisfy the primal urgency that seemed to have taken her over. She obligingly lifted her bottom to enable him to slide her jeans over her hips and down her legs. The truth be told, at that moment Tess would have agreed if he'd announced he were actually the true King of England.

'It feels natural,' she confided throatily as he stopped kissing her long enough to pull her top over her head.

Rafe was struck by the truth in her pleasing observation, but he was in too much of a hurry to slow down and tell her so. He didn't bother unclipping her bra, just pushed down the lacy fabric that concealed her breasts from his hungry view.

A greedy, guttural sound emerged from low in his throat as her engorged breasts sprang free from their confinement. The feral sound made all the fine hairs over her body stand on end. Her quivering thighs opened to accommodate the knee he placed on the edge of the table. The friction as his knee nudged the highly sensitised area between her legs made her gasp; it was a raw, fractured sound.

Either the faint noise had been abnormally amplified or his senses were highly attuned to her because Tess found his eyes immediately sought hers.

'Sorry, I was clumsy.' He made a minor adjustment that relieved the pressure.

'You're anything but clumsy,' she breathed appreciatively. 'And that's not flattery,' she added forcefully, 'it's fact!' she explained with fervour.

'I stand corrected.' He reached down and his fingers slowly slid under the lacy edge of her pants to touch the ultra-sensitive skin of her inner thigh. 'Did I hurt you here…?' He pushed the fabric aside and let his fingers touch the sweet, damp heat. His delicate, teasing touch pushed Tess to the very limit of pleasure and beyond; every muscle in her abdomen contracted in unison, she simply melted.

'So slick, so hot… You want this…you want me…?'

'That has to be the most ridiculous thing you've ever asked me!' she told him hoarsely.

He responded with a look so primitive and predatory that a low keening cry was wrenched from deep inside her.

'I…you, *please*, Rafe!' she panted.

Rafe didn't seem to have any trouble deciphering her inarticulate plea. For a moment he watched her pale body writhe sinuously beneath him. Then, with one foot still on the floor, his body curved fully over hers and he pushed her slowly backwards until she lay there with her hair spread out around her delicately flushed face.

His eyes moved hungrily over the slender contours of her almost naked body. Perversely the tiny scraps of lace stretched across her lower body and beneath her breasts made her appear more naked, more *his*.

He fought with the last dregs of his control to subdue the primitive desire to possess that stretched every nerve and sinew in his body to breaking-point. Slow and gentle had its place, but that place wasn't here and now. On the other hand he didn't want to spoil things by rushing her.

He watched with covetous, burning eyes the rise and fall of her deliciously rounded pink-tipped breasts. Slowly he touched the side of one quivering mound before his mouth moved hungrily to the rosy swollen peak.

The sight of his dark head against the pale skin of her breasts was the most erotic thing Tess had ever seen. She cried out as his tongue lashed and his lips expertly teased.

She lay there in a delicious sensual haze until the pleasure centres of her brain finally overloaded. She simply couldn't take any more of this! Frantically she clutched awkwardly at the smooth golden skin that covered his broad back. Her nails left raised red grooves as they slid down the powerful curve before coming to rest on the taut firmness of his behind.

'If you don't do something I'll die!' She genuinely believed what she said and it showed.

'You won't be alone,' he rumbled.

Tess was vaguely conscious of him adjusting his clothing before he slid his hands under her buttocks. She heard the sound of tearing fabric an instant before he settled between her legs; she felt the hard tip of his arousal against her belly. The stark reality of what she was about to do hit her then; what surprised her most was that it didn't scare her.

Fingernails inscribing small half-moons in the delicate flesh of her palms, she lifted her arms up over her head. 'I want to see...' There was stark appeal in the feverish eyes she lifted to his face. Intent on increasing the intimate contact, she shifted and rotated her hips restlessly beneath his.

Rafe covered her hands with his and pinioned them either side of her head. 'You want to see what...?'

'You.'

It was the most incredible thing to see him slide slowly into her, until to all intents and appearances they were one. It was even more incredible, not to mention indescribably pleasurable, that her body could accommodate him. She was sobbing from the wonder of it when she raised her eyes to his. If it never got any better than this, it was still the most marvellous she'd ever felt in her life.

'Is this the sort of something you had in mind?'

She shook her head—the words hadn't been invented that could accurately describe anything this mind-blowingly erotic! Besides, she didn't trust herself to open her mouth because she was experiencing an almost incapacitating desire to say she loved him.

'And this sort of something...?'

He began to move. Tess closed her eyes tightly as things began to get very much better indeed! She was never quite sure, but she thought she might have screamed something to that effect just before his slow thrusts—it seemed impossible that such a big man could move with such incredible controlled precision—became more vigorous. *Much* more vigorous.

Then there were no thoughts at all, just the fierce, primitive rhythm that swept her along until a shattering climax ripped through her. Barely seconds later she heard Rafe cry out and felt his release pulse deep within.

Now she was here she could understand why they'd both been in such a hurry to reach the journey's end.

CHAPTER SIX

'WHAT are you doing?' Tess protested as Rafe bundled her and as many stray items of clothing as came within his grasp up into his arms.

She'd been quite content—well, a bit more than content, actually—to lie there beneath his heavy, sweat-slick body and enjoy the extraordinary intimacy of the quiet following the storm.

And what a storm! Tess had never imagined she would find herself in a situation, or with a man, who could make her forget her natural inhibitions and behave with such wonderful, wanton abandon.

Control had never been something Tess had had to work hard at; she had buckets of the stuff. How could surrender be fulfilling erotically or otherwise? From her comfortable position of smug security she had never been able to understand how women of her acquaintance—women who in every other way were strong and confident—could allow and actively *desire* to surrender that control to a man. Now she knew...*boy, oh, boy, did she know*!

The memory of the driving, all-consuming need to be possessed still had an almost surreal quality to it. There was nothing surreal, however, about the warm ache of fulfilment that was snugly curled up low in her belly. The total belief that Rafe had been just as much a helpless victim of his desires as she had been of hers made her feel neither victim or defeated; in fact she'd never dreamt that this sort of fulfilment existed!

She was vaguely aware that she ought to feel embarrassed. Maybe I will, she mused, when I'm able to think about what happened with cold, clinical objectivity. Tess had never felt quite this far away from clinical objectivity in her life! Mellow didn't begin to describe the warm, satisfied glow that engulfed her. She'd never considered herself the uptight sort, but this was a new experience for her…and not the first of the day, she mused, a small smile tugging at the corners of her generous mouth.

'To bed.'

There was no sexual significance to his prosaic reply, but heat flooded her body. As foolish as it obviously was, she couldn't deny that the sound of his deep voice seemed to be enough to send a shudder of desire all the way down to her curling toes.

'Isn't that a bit like shutting the stable door after the horse has bolted?' She swallowed to lubricate the dryness of her throat, watching Rafe move to lock the door.

'Do you fancy any Tom, Dick or Harry walking in to find you stretched out on the kitchen table?' he enquired.

Tess felt the first stirrings of unease threaten to spoil her laid-back mood. And small wonder, she reflected. He'd managed to conjure up a painfully stark image.

'What a tasteless comment,' she complained.

'Crude but accurate.'

There was no arguing with that even though she'd have liked to.

Rafe used her silence to elaborate on his theme—quite unnecessarily, as far as she was concerned. 'Can you imagine how swiftly that story would spread around the village?'

Tess grimaced; she could. 'I'd have to move house.' She wasn't entirely joking.

'That might not be such a bad idea,' he observed cryptically just before he dumped her on the bed.

Tess lay there in an unselfconscious tangle of pale naked limbs puzzling over what he'd said. 'What do you mean?' she began.

It was the expression on Rafe's lean face as he looked down at her that made her lose the thread. It also made her intensely conscious of every inch of naked flesh she was casually flaunting.

Of course he was staring; she was female and naked. Given the opportunity, wouldn't most men stare at a naked woman? *Any* naked woman—*any* being the significant word here. Testosterone would win over manners every time.

'I wish you wouldn't look at me like that,' she fretted with a disapproving frown.

'Like what?' he asked, without shifting the focus of his attention.

'Like you're salivating.'

A laugh was wrenched from him. 'Not visibly, I hope?'

'You doing anything that wasn't aesthetically pleasing…I don't think so!' He had to be the most naturally elegant creature she'd ever laid eyes on, she decided. Furthermore his grace was totally unstudied, an intrinsic part of him. No wonder she often felt challenged in the grace department in his company. 'I'm sure you look pretty damned great with egg on your face.'

Even though her spiky observation sounded more like a criticism than a compliment, her eyes wore eating up every detail of his appearance. Tiny insignificant things delighted and fascinated her, like the oval-shaped mole just above his right nipple, and the way…dear God, Tess, anyone would think you were in love or something! Her eyes widened in acute anxiety. No, I can't be, not now…not with Rafe!

'You're very kind, but all the same that's a situation I prefer to avoid… Just to be on the safe side, you understand.'

Tess didn't respond to the whimsy.

'Are you all right?' Rafe frowned. The colour had fled so dramatically from her face that he thought for an uncomfortable couple of seconds she was going to pass out. Women didn't normally look as though they were about to throw up after he'd made love to them.

'I'm fine…absolutely fine!' Her voice cracked comically on the last syllable.

Her squeaking response didn't make Rafe smile; his angular jaw set stubbornly. He refused point-blank to believe that she was regretting what had happened. He wouldn't damn well let her!

'You have to expect a bit of drooling, Tess, when you're flaunting your beautiful body like this.' His fierce grin showed signs of strain just before Tess, unable to stand the exposure any longer, slid awkwardly under the covers, her cheeks burning.

A classic case of too little too late, she thought, feeling ridiculously gauche. It's not as if there is much he hasn't already seen, and even less he hasn't touched.

'That wasn't a complaint. However,' Rafe conceded with a regretful sigh, 'it will make it easier to talk, and we do need to talk.'

Easier for whom? she wondered. Rafe might have pulled on his trousers, though he hadn't stopped to fasten his belt, but he wasn't wearing his shirt. A face full of perfect pectorals made it hard for a girl to concentrate. Lust she could cope with, she told herself briskly—it was the other *L* word that made her jumpy.

'Talk…about what?' Not the start of a deep and meaningful relationship—that went without saying. She ignored the first stirrings of dissatisfaction in her breast. He was probably worried she'd start getting emotional and clingy, so now probably wasn't the moment to tell him.

'You don't have to worry, Rafe, I know it didn't mean anything.' She managed a creditably light-hearted smile. He looked unaccountably annoyed, which seemed pretty unreasonable even by his standards.

'I can see the attractions of your strategy,' he reflected thoughtfully.

Talk of *strategy* came as a surprise to Tess, who was

having trouble with the simplest of mental processes. 'What strategy?' she puzzled.

'If you think someone's about to kick you where it hurts, get the boot in first.'

To listen to him talk anyone would think she'd wounded him. She brushed aside that ludicrous piece of wishful thinking. 'Since when did you get so sensitive? I'm sorry if you think I was being too blunt, but it's a bit late in the day for us to start pretending.'

'That would be foolish,' he agreed gravely.

Tess bit her lip. He was literally oozing polite disbelief. 'I'm trying to keep this as painless as possible,' she reproached. 'There's bound to be a bit of…awkwardness involved when you sleep with someone you've been friends with. I'm only trying to make this easier for you. I'm sure you've got too much on your plate to want any added *complications*—I know I have.'

Right now she needed to devote all her energy to the Ben dilemma. There had never been a less appropriate time to pursue her own selfish pleasures. 'At least we don't have to worry about unwanted pregnancies.' Smiling about this was one of the hardest things she'd ever done. And what did she get for her efforts…? He didn't even look relieved.

'Actually, I've no interest in debating how empty and meaningless you found our love-making.'

'Don't put words into my mouth!' she protested.

'Now there's a sentiment I can identify with,' Rafe came back grimly. He fixed her with a stern, unblinking stare and wasted no more time before introducing the subject that had been and still was uppermost in his mind. 'The celibacy thing…just what sort of time scale are we talking here?' he enquired with deceptive casualness.

Nothing could have sounded more offhand than her response…possibly too offhand, she worried. 'A while…' She threaded the fringe of the brightly coloured throw around her finger before arranging it in an artistically pleasing pattern against the white sheet.

'A *long* while…? Will you stop doing that?' he rapped abruptly, snatching the material from her restless fingers and seating himself on the side of the bed.

'It might be,' she conceded defiantly.

He watched the flicker of emotion run across her deeply expressive face and cursed. It didn't seem possible, but deep down he'd known that against all the odds he was right! Worse still, part of him—the politically incorrect, Neanderthal part—had felt a primitive gloating delight at the notion of being the first.

'There's no need to swear!'

Rafe thought there was every need. 'A long time as in never?' He hit his forehead with his hand before dragging it through his thick mop of glossy dark hair. The expression on her face had said it all!

'And if it is?' she challenged, lifting her hot-cheeked face to his. 'So what? There's certainly no need to hold an inquest.'

'We'll have to agree to differ on that one.'

'So what's new?' she flung at him carelessly. 'Since when have we ever agreed on anything?' He was the most unreasonable person she knew. Being friends is hard enough—whatever made me think that being lovers would work out any better? That argument lost its validity when she reluctantly acknowledged that *thinking* hadn't had a whole lot to do with it at the time! Now, if you were talking blind lust, compulsion, frenzied urgency…

Rafe's chiselled nostrils flared as his sensual lips thinned. 'I can't believe you gave away something you obviously valued so highly so casually!'

Was Rafe of all people lecturing her on morals?

'It wasn't casual!' she yelled, coming up onto her knees and drawing the sheet with her up to her chin.

The wariness in his sharp glance made her realise how easily what she had said could be misinterpreted...or not...?

'I didn't mean *casual* exactly,' she contradicted swiftly. 'I meant this was different...obviously.'

'Obviously?' he enquired unsmilingly.

'It had been a very stressful twenty-four hours for us both.' She gave an exasperated sigh as a stony-faced Rafe failed to display any appreciation of the point she was trying to make. 'A series of freak circumstances.'

'Not to mention insatiable lust.'

'All right!' she exclaimed. 'Insatiable lust. There! Does that make you feel any better?' He'd made her feel better—a *lot* better, and now he was spoiling it with this interrogation. 'It's not like I was waiting for Mr Right or anything,' she assured him scornfully.

'Well, you wouldn't be, would you?' he bit back.

'Am I supposed to know what the hell you're getting at?'

'I'm saying the victim look does nothing for you,' he announced brutally.

'I don't think of myself like that!' Tess exclaimed, genuinely horrified that anyone could think she cultivated a martyred attitude.

'*No?*' Rafe's dark brows arched sceptically. 'You talk like you're some sort of cripple...not quite a *whole* woman.'

His accusation stung. 'I'm just being realistic. I'm sorry if it makes you feel uncomfortable.'

'Realistic!' Rafe found himself responding furiously. 'Self-pitying, more like, but don't expect me to make any concessions for your *disability*! Thousands of people live perfectly productive, happy lives with *real* disabilities. You can't have a baby—'

'*So what!*' she jumped in. How could a man, especially one as selfish and insensitive as Rafe, begin to understand? 'Is that what you're saying?'

'I'm saying that it's tough and unfair, but then that's life. The fact you can't have babies is part of what you are, like the colour of your eyes, it's not *who* you are.' His voice had become surprisingly gentle and Tess felt her throat grow tight with emotion. 'There's always adoption...?' Two slashes of colour stained the sharp angle of his cheekbones as he watched her blink back the tears that sparkled in those vulnerable green depths. 'Anyhow, you certainly felt all woman to me.' His abrupt tone suggested she'd done this just to aggravate him.

'I did?' Hell, why don't you just start purring, Tess? she asked herself bitterly. He's just virtually designated you an emotional disaster area and all you can think about is some throw-away remark that he probably only added to make you feel better!

She hardened her heart and her expression before she looked directly at him. 'Pardon me,' she said coldly, 'if I don't take advice from a man who thinks it's a good idea to fall in love with a married woman!' Remorse washed over her the instant the words were out of her mouth.

Eyes coldly angry, he grinned humourlessly back at her, displaying a set of perfect, even whiter than white teeth. 'You do go for the jugular, don't you, angel?'

'I'm sorr—'

'Don't apologise, you're right. I think the children tipped the balance in the end.' If she was going to look at him as though he was a moral degenerate, he might as well give her the opportunity to look all the way down her cute nose— yes, it is, isn't it? he realized, looking at her small tip-tilted appendage with a surge of affection tinged with definite lust.

That had always been the way of it with Tess. One minute you wanted to strangle her—his eyes darkened as they automatically flickered to the smooth, pale length of her slender throat—the next you wanted... Rafe stiffened. Actually, until very recently he'd never wanted to do *that* before.

'She has children...?' Tess gasped, looking shocked enough to fulfil even his cynical expectations.

'Two. But aren't we straying off the subject? Now, let me think…what was it? I know, virginity.'

'I wish you'd leave it alone,' she breathed wearily. 'The fact is, I'm not terribly highly sexed.'

There wasn't even a trace of irony in her grave explanation. Rafe threw back his head and laughed. There was still mirth in his eyes when he'd managed to compose himself; the slashing white grin disappeared in deference to her icy disapproval.

'You're a tonic, Tess.'

'I'm so glad I've managed to brighten your day,' she responded frigidly.

Not to mention complicate my life, he amended silently. He had a gut certainty—Rafe relied heavily on gut certainty—that there were ramifications to this he hadn't even thought of yet!

'It's not like I've been deliberately holding onto it or anything. Actually,' she continued, 'I was in a fairly serious relationship and was on the point of…giving it away, as you so tastefully phrase it,' she snapped, 'when the doctor told me about…that I couldn't…you know… I told Tom. It wasn't as if we were going to get married or anything, but I thought he had the right to know.' A faraway look entered her wide-spaced eyes as she recalled the events of five years earlier.

'And *Tom* did what?' Rafe asked in that deceptively languid tone.

'He said he was sorry, but…'

'The creep dumped you!' Rafe ground out savagely.

Tess shrugged. 'Illness really freaked him out. I know I wasn't ill, precisely, but he—'

'Now I know where you got all these bloody stupid ideas from.'

'Don't be silly, Rafe. I'm not denying I was hurt at the time, but it doesn't matter now. He did me a favour really—'

'You mean he jumped off the nearest high building?' Rafe

smiled in what Tess considered a sinister, scary way as he contemplated this scenario.

Rafe could make sinister look not only scary, but *sexy* too... Tess instinctively knew it would be a bad idea to follow that thought to its conclusion, especially when all she had to do was reach out to touch acres of golden firm flesh...

She jammed quivering fingertips under her knee and ran her tongue over the outline of her dry lips. 'I mean,' she explained brusquely, 'that it made me see how pointless it would be to get seriously involved with anyone when there could be no future. I thought about casual sex,' she confessed.

'Don't we all?' he came back flippantly. Didn't casual imply a fun, relaxed, no headaches, no emotional trauma situation? The throb in his temples kicked up another notch as she began to idly chew a stray strand of rich reddish-tinged hair.

Once she'd even gone so far as to go clubbing with a friend whose idea of a good night out was to pick up an able and willing male—*any* able and willing male! It had taken Tess about half an hour to realise that it wasn't the route for her to go. She could think of better ways to prove she was as liberated as a man!

'Only I haven't got the stomach for it.'

'Until now.'

'That was different.' She gritted her teeth and wished he'd stop being so tiresome about the entire business.

'So you keep saying. Why? That's what I want to know.'

Don't we all? 'I suppose you think I should have told you? The fact is, I didn't even think about it...actually, I wasn't thinking at all,' she amended wryly, recalling with a deep blush the frantic urgency that had gripped her. 'Except about...you know...' She looked self-consciously away.

'I know, all right,' he conceded drily. A man who had slept with a vulnerable virgin ought to feel like a first-class heel—Rafe had—but that feeling was fading fast as his sexual interest was being stirred…actually, *stirred* was a pretty anaemic description of the prowling hunger that was beginning to twist his guts into tortuous knots. He suddenly had a strong mental picture of some other faceless male taking over where he'd left off and the muscles in his belly cramped hard in fierce rejection. It wasn't in his nature to leave anything half finished.

'It honestly wasn't an issue for me. I don't feel defiled or anything daft like that.' With a laugh designed to illustrate how lacking she was in neuroses, Tess firmly rejected this idea. 'If you must know I feel liberated…empowered, even!' she elaborated, resorting to a humorously extravagant gesture. The gesture fell flat on its face at approximately the same moment the sheet slid down to her waist. She didn't feel particularly empowered as she scrabbled to pull it up again. 'I should have done it years ago,' she gritted with determined and audibly forced humour.

Rafe was watching her with that dark, brooding, enigmatic expression of his.

'All you had to do was ask.'

Tess's laughter was genuine this time, if tinged with bitterness. 'What a whoppa!' she gasped. 'You've never fancied me even slightly.' Which was probably the only reason their friendship had survived past puberty! 'See,' she jeered, wagging her finger at him. 'You can't deny it!'

He caught her finger and, holding her eyes with his own, raised it to his lips. He kissed the tip softly before he drew it slowly into his mouth. He sucked.

All her stomach muscles, including the deep neglected ones, contracted in unison. Tess's eyes darkened dramatically as she gave a deep, voluptuous sigh.

'I keep telling you some things change.'

Not the sexiness of his voice…that was one of life's eternal features. 'Not *that* much,' she croaked in a dazed, resentful whisper as she snatched her damp finger away. She suspected he was making fun of her.

'Then why,' he enquired with unforgivable insight, 'are you trembling?'

'I'm not saying you're not attractive—especially,' she added drily, 'when you try so hard.' Why, she wondered a little hazily, was he trying at all?

'If you think that was trying, angel...'

'All right, all right,' she responded, anxious to avoid any and all demonstrations of Rafe's seductive powers. 'Let's take your stud status as read, shall we?' she offered sweetly.

'Cow!' he countered affectionately.

'When I needed someone, you were there.' And even if she had been the type to waste her tears over spilt milk, Tess knew she would never regret it. 'But now is different.'

'Now you know what you're doing,' he suggested quietly.

'Exactly.' She couldn't help but feel slightly regretful that she was in full possession of her senses.

'I'm going to remind you that you said that,' he responded cryptically. 'The next time we make love,' he added, not at all cryptically, in response to her puzzled expression.

'You're not suggesting we...we do this sort of thing on a...a...'

'Regular basis?' The metal bed-frame shuddered as he disposed his long, lean frame comfortably beside her. 'I can't think of any sensible reason not to.'

'I can. I can think of several hundred!'

'I said a *sensible* reason. We both have needs which are not being fulfilled anywhere else at the moment.'

'As propositions go, that has all the old-fashioned charm of a demographic survey! I'm damned if I'm going to make myself available for you when you just happen to be in the area. It's so *demeaning*.' Tess gave a little shudder of distaste and didn't notice he'd grown rigid with anger. 'I think what you need is a good old-fashioned mistress!'

Abruptly Rafe rolled over onto his side and firmly removed the sheet from her white-knuckled grasp; equally firmly he took hold of her slim thigh and tugged her down until they lay face to face. His eyes burnt with fierce determination as they swept over the slender length of her trembling body before coming to rest on her face.

'What I need is you.'

Heat flooded her belly; tiny red dots danced before her eyes.

'And you need me,' he announced with equal authority. 'I know we didn't go out looking for this to happen, but it has.' He felt the tremor run through her body as he cupped one soft breast in his big hand. 'I certainly wasn't looking to forget my problems in some sort of sexual frenzy,' he admitted hoarsely.

Frenzy! Had he really said frenzy? Tess was having trouble focusing on his lean dark face. She had never thought of herself as the type of female capable of inspiring frenzy in anyone. It was satisfying to have it confirmed that she hadn't been the only one to feel that way. She squirmed and said his name softly as his thumb rubbed gently over her tight, rigid nipple.

His next words suggested that Rafe was equally puzzled by this bizarre occurrence. 'Neither was I expecting to find myself feeling this sort of attraction for anyone so soon—if ever—least of all you!'

Tess looked as though she had a nasty taste in her mouth. She was furious with herself for lying there passively letting him touch her how he wanted. Deep down, the idea of letting Rafe touch her how he wanted—how *she* wanted—was a dizzyingly exciting prospect.

She placed her hands on his shoulders and pushed hard, but to little effect. 'That's where I have the advantage, Rafe,' she puffed. 'I've always known you were shallow, but I can see the discovery has come as something of a shock to you...'

'You could have some great fun exploring my shallows,' he promised with a wicked gleam in his eyes.

Tess gave a worried groan and stopped trying to budge

his muscular bulk. 'Don't you think this is getting a bit...*heavy* for a harmless flirtation?' she worried.

'It got heavy for me about the same time you started to rip off my clothes.'

He had been pretty active on the ripping front, and Tess wasn't about to take the entire rap. 'You were the one ripping.'

'Talking of which.' He reached behind her and clicked free the crumpled bra which had stopped being supportive some time before. He held up the scrap of black lace before dropping it to the floor.

'You're obviously on the rebound' she suggested, trying to sound confident and slightly amused about this. Her failure to sound anything but shakily breathless was mostly due to the fact his right arm had smoothly settled into a possessive position over her hip. His fingers moved restlessly over the soft skin of her modestly rounded behind. Her words might have had more impact if she hadn't responded so enthusiastically to the long, languid kiss he pressed to her slightly parted lips.

'Far less dangerous to rebound in your direction, Tess, than a stranger who might think...'

'It meant anything,' she finished dully, drawing the back of her hand angrily over her just-kissed lips. She couldn't wipe away the taste of him from her mouth.

'Of course it means something.' His fingers moved in a series of graceful, gentle arabesques along the projections of her spine. Desire sharp and sweet clutched deep inside her. 'It means I want you, and you want me.'

'Aren't you presuming...?' Under her half-closed eyelids she watched with a sense of helplessness Rafe examine her aching breasts as they visibly responded to his statement. Small wonder he looked pretty smug!

'Am I?'

It was an inconvenient time to discover she couldn't look

him in the eye and lie. 'You make it sound uncomplicated and simple...'

Even while she was protesting, she had the feeling they both knew she was just going through the motions. Some things in life were inevitable and she'd discovered pretty late on in hers that one of them was when Rafe said he wanted her she was a lost cause! Could this be a genetic flaw? she wondered.

'It's nothing of the sort. So far all we've done is argue and fight...'

'We *always* argue and fight.'

'And normally I don't give a damn.'

She saw a thoughtful expression drift into his eyes. Stifling a cry of vexation, she bit her tongue until she tasted the tang of salt. 'Listen, Rafe,' she said, grabbing a pillow from above her head and pushing it between them. It hurt her sensitised breasts and it made a puny defence, but it was better than nothing. 'I value our friendship, but it'll never survive us...'

'Being lovers? Aren't you being just the tiniest bit perverse? One minute all we do is argue and fight, the next our friendship is worth preserving at any cost...including my sanity!' he growled.

Shock made her forget how imperative it was not to look directly at him. It took about two seconds of exposure to that dark, smouldering glare to almost paralyse her with desire.

'You should go visit your grandfather.' She found it hard to form the words. 'I should...'

'Sit here all alone and brood. I think my idea is better. You know how to wound a bloke, Tess. Here I am offering you my body and my not inconsiderable expertise...'

He might have made it sound like a joke, but Rafe was deadly serious. He knew she'd enjoyed their first frantic coupling; her reactions had been more eloquent than any lavish words of praise. Rafe found he wanted to teach—to hell with want! He *needed* to show her the finer subtleties, show her how good restraint could be. He'd be so damned restrained that she'd be begging him to take her, he decided, smiling with grim determination into her flushed, aroused face! He might do a bit of begging himself, just to show her there wasn't a damned thing wrong with it.

Just when his own was climbing to explosion-point, the strain faded from Tess's face and she burst out laughing. 'Why, you...!'

Rafe grabbed the pillow she'd just whacked him over the head with. 'That wasn't just an idle boast.' Tess found the combination of warm laughter and smouldering awareness in his eyes tremendously potent and attractive. The smile faded from her face.

'I'm sure you've been around, but spare me the details.'

'Compared to you, Tess, a newborn kitten has been around, but I'm here to change all that.' He took her chin between his thumb and forefinger and refused to let her look away.

'I don't think I want anything to change.'

'What are you going to do—pretend we didn't make love? Pretend you didn't enjoy it? Pretend you don't want to repeat the experience just as much as I do?' He shook his head reprovingly from side to side. 'Too much pretending for one woman. Break the habit of a lifetime, Tess. Live for the moment, lover...'

'That's a very dangerous philosophy.' Attractive and extraordinarily tempting, she didn't add.

'You're a warm and sensual woman, Tess.'

She knew it wasn't true, but Rafe had a very authoritative way with words. The fact his hand was expertly caressing her breast again probably helped the illusion along slightly too!

Tess felt as if she were dissolving along with her doubts. 'Was it *very* obvious, Rafe?' she whispered, unable to restrain her curiosity any longer. His thumb moved across her nipple and she moaned.

'It was obvious you were made to do this to me,' he responded huskily. 'God knows why I never realised it before.'

'Do what?'

'This.' He took her hand; Tess got the drift straight away.

'You feel...'

'Overdressed.'

'That too,' she conceded huskily.

'You could do something about that. Would you like to?' he asked, brushing the heavy swathe of hair from her hot cheek.

'I want to so much I can't breathe.' Her confession came in a rush and with much heavy breathing. His reply was music to her ears.

Rafe inhaled deeply, drawing the female fragrance of her deep into his lungs. 'You can do all the things you want to.' He continued to kiss her face and neck, sliding his fingers deep into her hair as he angled her chin first this way and then another until there seemed hardly a centimetre of skin his lips hadn't touched.

All she wanted to do was love him, this person she'd known almost all her life but had never really *seen* until today. Had she changed...? Had he...? Tess thought it didn't really matter. It mattered that she'd never been as sure of anything in her entire life. Not that it does me any good, she thought bleakly, when it's the one thing I'm not allowed to do.

'I'm not sure I know how.'

Rafe stopped playing at kissing and did it properly. Rafe's casual was way better than most people's best; his best was very good indeed! 'I know how, I'll show you. All you have to do is tell me what you want.'

'I couldn't do that,' she whispered.

'You've never run scared of telling me what's on your

mind before.' His thumb moved rhythmically over one tight, swollen nipple.

Tess gave a tortured moan. 'That's different.'

'Beautifully different, just like you.'

It was.

CHAPTER SEVEN

RAFE sat at the opposite end of the long table from his grandfather. The arrangement wasn't exactly intimate. You could have comfortably seated at least twenty people between them along the gleaming mahogany surface. In the past he'd frequently seen it accommodate at least that many people. The atmosphere had been convivial on those occasions; tonight it was not.

He toyed with the empty crystal goblet beside his plate. 'Do you eat in here when you're alone?'

'Some of us like to maintain standards.' Edgar Farrar looked with thinly veiled disapproval at his grandson's casual attire. His grandfather's disapproval had stopped bothering Rafe a long time before. 'What would you have me do—eat on a tray in front of the television?'

Rafe's lips twitched. What a scandalous thought! He had noticed the old man's colour had got progressively darker through the meal as he'd accepted the wine his grandson had refused...drinking for two? Rafe wondered how the old man's blood pressure was behaving these days. He didn't ask—he didn't think his concern would be well received. He supposed the ironic thing was that he did actually feel concerned.

'Yeah, the dreaded telly, it's really killed the art of conversation, hasn't it?' Rafe drawled, his sarcasm pronounced. They'd sat through four courses and not exchanged more than half a dozen words before the coffee stage.

I'd have been better off staying at the cottage with Tess, he thought, not for the first time. Actually he would have stayed if she hadn't forcibly expelled him, insisting she wanted to cope with Chloe without any distractions.

111

'Heard from Dad lately?'

His father had been living in luxurious exile with his wife in the South of France since he'd been caught with his fingers in the till. Actually, the embezzlement had been a little more sophisticated than that—Guy Farrar might be greedy and impatient, but he was also clever. Not as clever as his father, though, it turned out.

When he'd discovered the crime Edgar had used his own money to cover the theft and set about limiting the damage. He'd succeeded. Inevitably there had been rumours but the family honour had survived the incident intact, which Rafe pondered cynically, was all that mattered! This done, Edgar had told his son he was no longer welcome in the country. Guy had known that Edgar had the power to make life very uncomfortable if he hadn't obeyed the edict.

Rafe didn't regret his parent's departure, but he did feel a twinge of remorse as the older man's ruddy colour intensified.

Despite all the odds, he felt an affection for the bigoted, intolerant old despot which he had never felt for his own father or, for that matter, his brother. His mother had been tearfully delighted to see him when he'd sought her out just after his eighteenth birthday, but you couldn't turn back the clock. Rafe didn't resent this. He knew she had a new family to consider, and he was genuinely happy she'd found someone to make her happy. No, he and Edgar were stuck with each other.

It was probably cruel to bait his grandfather, but then, he reflected wryly, the old man always had been a lifelong advocate of blood sports!

'I hear from your father. He worries I've disinherited him.' Edgar's heavy-hooded lids lifted and he gave a thin-lipped smile.

'And have you?' Rafe wondered casually.

'You'd like that, wouldn't you?' Edgar accused.

'If you think I give a damn one way or the other about

your money and this estate, you couldn't be more wrong,' Rafe told him without heat.

Edgar Farrar's face betrayed the frustration he felt knowing the boy only spoke the truth.

The shrill buzz of his mobile interrupted Rafe's thoughts, which had already wandered in the direction of Walnut Cottage.

Under his grandfather's austere gaze he fished the phone from his pocket.

'Tess.' He could see her so clearly she could have been standing here in front of him. His nostrils twitched; he could almost smell the soft scent of her body. Taking into account the fact his imagination had failed to supply clothes, it was probably just as well—for his grandfather's continued mental well-being—that the image remained a product of his fertile, not to mention erotic imagination.

Rafe was shocked by the degree of pleasure he felt at hearing her voice. He was even more shocked by the way his body reacted lustfully. The pleasure rapidly faded as he registered the anxiety in her voice.

'Blood group…?' His brows drew together in a perplexed troubled line as he supplied the information she requested. 'You know I have. As rare as hen's teeth, so they tell me.' He recited parrot-like the constituents of his rare blood group. His expression darkened as he listened to the babbled explanation. 'The infirmary—I'll be there.' He glanced at the metallic watch on his wrist. 'Twenty…no, make that fifteen minutes.'

'Did you know…?' he rapped, surging to his feet. Struggling to contain his anger, he towered over the older man looking forbidding.

'Know what?' Edgar Farrar wasn't used to being looked at as if he were a particularly nasty bug; he didn't like it.

For once Rafe could find no redeeming humour in the old man's sneering attitude; the joke of being the object of his grandfather's distaste had abruptly vanished.

'Know that your precious Alec had fathered a bastard of one of the local maidens.' One of the only things he'd ever had in common with his deceased elder brother was an extremely rare blood group. It seemed his brother had passed that same blood group on to his son Ben, who was now awaiting surgery in the local city hospital. Tess must be beside herself... He wanted to be there with her; he didn't want to waste time here with the old man.

Edgar Farrar shot to his feet, his arthritic knee forgotten. His eyes blazed. *'How dare you?'*

'Sure,' Rafe drawled, throwing his jacket over his shoulder. 'You shouldn't speak ill of the dead and he was worth ten of me, but don't say you didn't know my sainted brother habitually cheated on poor Annabel.' He laughed harshly as fresh colour suffused his grandfather's already ruddy cheeks. 'Sure you knew, but he cheated with such exquisite discretion and good taste you turned a blind eye.'

'Where do you think you're going, boy?' Edgar yelled at the ramrod straight back of his only remaining grandson. 'Do you think I'd have ignored a child of Alec's if I knew he existed!'

The quaver in the old man's voice made Rafe pause. He slowed and turned back. 'Any heir would be preferable to me, is that right?' He searched the old man's face. 'I thought so.'

'Rafe!'

'Shut up! If I don't get to the hospital soon you won't have an heir at all!' he flung angrily over his shoulder.

It was the first time in his life that anyone had ever told Edgar Farrar to shut up. It took him several moments to recover from the shock, but recover he did.

'You really can't get up yet, Mr Farrar,' a young nurse protested weakly as Rafe swung his long legs over the side of the narrow bed.

'No, he can't,' the older and coolly imperious uniformed

figure who had escorted Tess into the cubicle agreed. 'I've no desire to spend my evening filling in accident forms in triplicate after you fall flat on your face.'

After a short pause Rafe, whose head had done some spectacular spinning as he'd sat up, complied with a rueful grin.

'Right, I'll send along a nice cup of tea and biscuits and you'll feel yourself in no time,' she said briskly, withdrawing with the younger nurse in her wake.

They just looked at one another. Tess knew she had to do something…say something… You couldn't tell a man what she had told Rafe and leave it like that.

'Fancy meeting you here,' Rafe drawled as Tess moved awkwardly forward. 'Any more secrets stored within that delightful bosom?' His eyes lifted from the heaving outline and he saw colour suffuse her face.

Tess sighed regretfully. 'I'm sorry I hit you with it like that, but things were a bit urgent.'

'How's the boy?'

He sounded as if he cared… What am I thinking? If he didn't care he wouldn't be here, she chided herself. 'He's in the operating theatre,' she explained huskily. 'They'll probably have to remove his spleen…' she caught her lower lip savagely between her teeth and continued huskily '…but he should be all right; thanks to you.'

'And the others?'

'Chloe had a nasty bang on the head, but it's only concussion. She should be able to go home in the morning. The driver of the lorry is suffering from shock, which isn't surprising. It must be a nightmare having your brakes pack up on you like that.'

'Sit here.' Rafe rolled onto his side, lifted his head and patted the side of the narrow bed he lay on. 'You look all in.'

Perhaps it was the trauma of the past hour or so, but the

gentleness in his voice brought an emotional lump to Tess's throat.

'Did they take much...?' She glanced warily at the plaster mark on his arm and took him up on his offer.

Actually she was glad to sit down. Her metabolic rate had been in a head-spinning, upward spiral ever since she'd received the phone call from a distraught Ian telling her about the accident. While she'd had something to do, namely get Rafe here to donate his all important blood, she'd been able to cope. Now all that was left was the waiting and she felt so tense a sharp word might be enough to make her crack wide open.

'The odd armful or two. Do I look pale and interesting?'

Actually he looked so devastatingly handsome that her heart had almost leapt from her chest the instant she'd seen him lying there.

'More pallid and pasty.' Tess heard the tremulous quiver in her voice and decided she might leave the sparkling repartee until she was more than one step away from being a basket case. She raised a self-conscious hand to her cheek. 'That probably makes two of us. It was lucky I remembered about your odd blood group.'

'I prefer rare, actually.'

'You had your blood frozen in case it was needed when you had that knee surgery a few years back, didn't you?'

'They do keep some in cold storage for me,' Rafe agreed.

'When they told me about Ben's I realised straight away it must be the same one...'

'Considering our close relationship,' he put in quietly.

'I knew you'd be mad with me.' Worriedly she searched his face and discovered he was searching hers just as diligently.

'For not mentioning in passing that I'm actually Ben's uncle?' The truth was he'd been planning on demanding an explanation from her, but one look at the wary, worried expression on her pale little face and his rancour had vanished leaving an urgent desire…no, actually, *overwhelming* came a lot closer to describing his desire to enfold her in a comforting embrace that would wipe the lines of worry from her brow.

'I don't know what I am with you, angel,' he admitted abruptly. 'I know I'm mad with Alec. Lucky for him he's dead,' he reflected, his eyes glowing with contempt as he thought about his late and unlamented brother. 'He always was a randy sod, but I didn't think even he would stoop that low…*my mistake*,' he added drily as Tess rested her forehead against his.

With a sigh Tess slipped off her shoes and cuddled up properly beside him. It was a relief to her he had taken the accuracy of what she'd told him for granted. He could have got understandably irked if he'd just thought she was bad-mouthing a dead man who couldn't defend himself. But then Rafe knew better than most that his brother had not been a nice man; in fact it was pretty obvious to her that she couldn't despise Alec any more than Rafe obviously did.

Her perfume was a pleasant change from the antiseptic hospital smell. Rafe inhaled deeply; he wasn't sure if she found it soothing to have her hair stroked, but he found it soothing doing the stroking.

'There's probably a rule about this sort of thing.'

'Considering the overstretched state of the National Health Service, bed-sharing could well be the way forward.'

Tess smiled weakly and rubbed her cheek against the hand he'd lifted to brush her hair from her eyes. 'Perhaps I'll just lie here for a moment. I can't actually do anything just now and they'll tell me if…'

'Sure they will,' he agreed in a soothing voice.

'I shouldn't have let him out of my sight.' Her voice was muffled against his shoulder.

His hand went to the back of her head. Rafe took a deep breath. How were you meant to console someone who sounded pretty damned inconsolable?

'I expect every parent thinks that when anything happens to their kid…and don't start with that "I'm just a distant relative" routine!'

'I just wish it was me lying…' Her voice cracked, before she ruthlessly stilled her trembling lip. She saved the luxury of tears for later when Ben was well again.

'I don't!'

A vision of Tess lying crumpled and broken like a rag doll on some roadside flashed before Rafe's eyes; he felt physically sick. He became conscious that some of his revulsion must have shown in his voice—Tess was staring at him oddly. He cleared his throat.

'Exchange isn't a solution in these cases,' he informed her drily. 'What the hell had Chloe seen in Alec anyhow? Silly question—the same as all the others did, I suppose.'

'She was very young and you can't deny he was *extremely* good-looking.'

'God, not you too!'

Tess had always disliked intensely the elder Farrar for trying to belittle his younger brother on every possible occasion. Even back then Rafe had been remarkably self-contained. It must have infuriated Alec that Rafe had risen above his sly jibes; it had also made him more vicious. Some people had seen the charm when they'd met Alec; Tess had seen that streak of viciousness.

'I thought he was a first-class sleaze,' she responded indignantly as she lifted her head from his shoulder. 'And you have to take your share of the blame in this.'

'Me!'

'Well, Chloe only turned her attention to Alec when you didn't co-operate. Don't tell me you didn't know she fancied you something rotten.'

'I knew, all right,' he conceded, looking uncomfortable as he recalled some of her attempts to gain his attention. 'And I'd sooner—! Well, shall we just say she's not my type?'

Tess couldn't let this assertion pass without comment. 'I'd have said she was *exactly* your type…tall, leggy and blonde.' She suddenly felt acutely the lack of all these attributes.

'You seem to have made an in-depth study of the subject,' he mused, taking her chin in his fingers and turning her face up to him.

Tess didn't want to expand further on that theme; she tugged her head away. 'Actually, I'm pretty sure Chloe imagined he'd leave Annabel and marry her,' she explained grimly.

'At least his death spared her a very nasty wake-up call,' Rafe rasped. A puzzled frown puckered his brow. 'Knowing Chloe's big romance with materialism, I'm just amazed she hasn't been milking Grandfather for money.'

'Chloe isn't *that* avaricious,' she protested stoutly.

'If you say so.'

'Actually,' Tess admitted awkwardly, 'she thinks she is…well, not *milking* exactly.' She raised herself up on her elbow and tucked a hank of floppy hair behind her ears. 'There's an annuity for her from the capital she *thinks* your grandfather provided…'

'And he didn't…'

'Gran never touched any of the money Mum and Dad left me for my education, and even after the taxman had his cut I did make quite a lot when I was working…'

'No wonder you seem strapped for cash.' Rafe shook his head in astonishment. 'Why the hell, Tess…?'

'My thought exactly. Run away, girl.' They hadn't noticed the two people enter the cubicle. The young nurse, even more overawed by the older generation of Farrar than she had been the younger, vanished like a worried rabbit. Edgar's gimlet gaze fixed on Tess. 'I assumed you were the mother…'

'No…no, I…Chloe…'

'Tess thought Alec was a sleaze,' Rafe explained succinctly, coming to Tess's rescue. 'You'd better make it quick, Grandfather—that poor kid has probably gone for reinforcements,' Rafe predicted, nodding after the retreating student nurse. Tess wondered how he could sound so calm. 'Or maybe it's just tea she's gone for. They did promise me some, not to mention biscuits. Shall I ask for another cup, Grandfather?'

'Spare me your savage wit, and don't get up on my account,' Edgar Farrar drawled as Tess, painfully conscious of how she must appear, tried to scramble off the bed. A strong and determined arm prevented her.

'We won't,' Rafe promised, his eyes coldly derisive as they clashed with his grandfather's.

'Well, girl?' the old man rapped.

'She's not a girl, she's a woman...she's *my* woman.' Rafe made it sound as if it made all the difference in the world, and of course it did—at least to Tess's world...or it would have if he'd meant it.

Tess knew Rafe's retort had really been intended to wind up, aggravate and generally provoke his grandfather—he never could resist an opportunity. Despite this, his words hit Tess just as hard in their own way as the lorry had hit Ian's car earlier that evening. The dramatic impact swept away the last wispy doubts she'd managed to retain; she wanted to be Rafe's girl, his woman, his *love*.

She wanted it for real because she loved him just about as much as it was possible for a woman to love a man. Strange that, even though she had very little personal experience of such things, Tess knew in every cell of her body that this was the for ever sort of love... Or, in this case, the hopeless, unrequited sort of love, she reminded herself brutally.

His grandfather's narrowed eyes moved over the two figures entwined on the bed. 'I'm not blind, boy,' he snapped. 'And I don't care who she is, I still demand to know what she thought she was about denying me my great-grandson.'

I won't bother asking why you're conniving with her...' he drawled contemptuously.

His contempt made Tess's face harden; she suddenly felt purposeful, not embarrassed. Rafe was worth a hundred of any Farrar alive or dead, and yet they all persisted in treating him appallingly! She touched the side of Rafe's face; it felt different somehow to look at him and know she loved him and always would.

'It's fine,' she murmured, wondering if she looked as different as she felt.

'Sure?'

Tess nodded firmly. This time he allowed her to rise.

She faced the figure who even now was much feared and revered in financial circles with a militant light in her blazing eyes.

'I didn't tell you for several reasons. Firstly I liked Annabel.' Alec's wife had been a sweet woman who had obviously thought her husband had been perfect. Even before his death she'd been devastated by her inability to supply him an heir; to learn Chloe had been expecting his child would have been one blow too many for the grieving widow.

A lot of people apart from Annabel seemed to think Alec had been perfect, Tess reflected, glaring at Rafe's grandfather as she angrily compared his attitude towards his two grandsons.

'She was always nice to me and I didn't want her to be hurt. Secondly—' her voice shook as she glared contemptuously at Edgar Farrar '—I'd seen how unhappy your household had made one young boy...' Her eyes softened momentarily as she looked back quickly over her shoulder at Rafe, before narrowing to emerald ice-chips again as she squared up to his grandfather. 'I'd no reason to believe you'd do any better the second time around,' she announced scornfully.

Rafe looked on in amazement as his grandfather flinched

and looked away from those critical, unforgiving green eyes. He doubted Tess realised what a rare thing she was seeing.

'Rafe was…is my son's responsibility,' he blustered uncomfortably. 'It wasn't my place to interfere with Guy.' This statement lacked his habitual assurance and it seemed from his expression he was conscious of the fact.

'Can I have that in writing?' Rafe muttered. He wasn't surprised when both combatants ignored him.

'I don't know who I despise more,' Tess announced, her clear voice ringing with scorn. 'Those people who beat children or those who know about it and do nothing!' She thought maybe she'd gone too far when Edgar gasped and clutched at his chest. 'Are you all right?' she cried anxiously.

'Sit down, Grandfather,' Rafe instructed sharply, rising from his sickbed with an athletic bound and taking charge of the situation. 'Shall I call a doctor?'

'Don't be stupid, I just need my pills!' Edgar drew a bottle from his breast pocket with tremulous fingers. 'That's better,' he breathed a few moments later.

Tess was relieved to see the blue discoloration had faded from his lips.

'Your father is a weak fool,' he wheezed. 'When I found out what Guy was doing I told him if he ever laid a finger on you again I'd break every bone in his body.'

'And they say violence breeds violence,' Rafe remarked. Underneath the sarcasm Tess could see he was looking thoughtful.

'You've brought up this boy alone, I take it.' The shrewd old eyes moved momentarily towards Rafe. 'There is no husband, live-in lover…'

Tess shook her head before he came up with another phrase to describe her solitary state. 'So far there's just been Ben and me,' she confirmed cautiously. She wasn't sure she liked the way Edgar Farrar's thoughts were heading. 'Shouldn't you lie down?' she fretted, watching as Rafe be-

gan to pace about the tiny space like a caged animal.
'You've lost a lot of blood.'

'I didn't lose it, I gave it away.'

'And I'll never forget it!' she told him, her eyes shining
with gratitude.

He'd be finding out just *how* grateful later; Rafe felt
ashamed of the thought. 'Don't worry, I won't put up a fight
when you want to get me into bed later,' he promised. He
grinned unrepentantly as heat flooded her indignant face,
leaving it prettily pink. 'Only just now I feel like being on
my feet...'

Not if...*when*... The arrogance of the man was astounding. Almost as astounding as his scorching sex appeal. She
made a last-ditch effort to tear her bemused eyes from his
face.

'There's plenty of time for courting later, boy,' his grandfather remonstrated, listening to this interchange with a critical frown. 'Right now I've got more important matters to
discuss than your love life...'

'Talking about important matters.' Tess gave a distracted
frown and patted the pager they'd promised to activate when
Ben was out of theatre. 'It shouldn't be long—perhaps I
should go and wait upstairs...' She turned with a frown to
Rafe.

Edgar Farrar stared in startled disbelief at the slim young
woman who had so summarily dismissed him.

'I'll come with you.'

'You should be resting, and you can't leave your grandfather...'

'I'm not an invalid, I don't need a keeper!' Edgar Farrar
exploded. 'And in point of fact I'm not your grandfather
either!'

Rafe's lip curled in a sneer. 'Isn't that taking wishful
thinking too far?' he asked, pointedly tapping his distinctive
aquiline nose. An almost identical feature adorned his grand-

father's weather-worn features. 'This sort of evidence is kind of hard to deny.'

'I'm not trying to deny anything.' The old man pulled himself to his feet with difficulty; his eyes didn't leave the younger man's scornful face for an instant. 'I'm your father.'

Tess realised by a process of elimination that the startled gasp had emerged from her mouth; neither man had moved or made a sound. Rafe's face looked as though it were carved from stone, except stone didn't have a pulse and she could see one in his blue-veined temple pounding away like a piston as he stared fixedly back at the older man.

'My father is living in the South of France with his charming wife.'

'Guy isn't your father.'

Rafe shook his head. 'Is this some bizarre attempt—?' He broke off, his eyes on the older man's face. 'You're telling the truth, aren't you?' he grated. 'My God, you *bastard*, you slept with your own son's wife! You slept with my mother…' He closed his eyes and shook his head as though his brain just couldn't deal with the information. 'I was always convinced that you were behind her going away, but I never suspected why!'

Edgar visibly recoiled from the white-hot animosity that glowed in the younger man's eyes.

Tentatively Tess touched Rafe's arm. 'His heart…'

'What heart?' Rafe grated, dismissing her concern with a harsh laugh. 'Did—?' He stopped on the point of saying *father*. A humourless grin pulled at the corners of his mouth. 'Does he know?'

'Guy…?'

'Well, I'm not talking about Prince Charles.'

'Nobody knows but your mother and I. It would have destroyed him.'

'Is it just me, or does your concern come a bit late in the day?'

'You have to understand that we did what we thought was best.'

'Best for who?' Rafe blasted. 'I know now why she went away, something that I've never been able to understand, but why the hell did she leave me behind where nobody wanted me?'

'I wanted you with me.'

'Don't make me laugh.'

Edgar gritted his teeth and persisted in the face of his son's acid scorn. 'You were...you *are* a Farrar, it's your birthright. Your mother understood this. Eventually it became untenable for her to stay with Guy.'

'I didn't need you, and I didn't need a birthright, I needed my mother.'

His words pierced her heart. Tess wanted to go to him, but she knew that for now she had to remain a bystander.

'I've told you we only did what we thought was best at the time. If Guy had found out there would have been a terrible scandal. Your mother knew that, she wanted to protect you.'

Rafe's cynicism deepened. 'Scandal! Now that sounds like something I can believe.'

'You don't understand, boy...we...we fell in love,' Edgar blustered awkwardly.

Tess winced at the scathing expression on Rafe's dark, unforgiving face. 'Pause for ironic laughter?' he suggested. 'Some things are just not possible and making what you did sound noble and virtuous definitely comes under that heading!'

'It was only the once. She was lonely and desperately unhappy.'

'And you were a bastard. I forgot—that's me, isn't it?'

'I'm not proud—'

'Of fathering such a disappointment...yeah...I'd sort of gathered that over the years.'

'I'm not proud of what I did to your...to Guy...to your

mother…to you. I felt guilty. I can see in retrospect that in trying to compensate for what I did I might have indulged Guy, and Alec. I didn't want to show you any preferential treatment.'

'You succeeded.'

'Alec wasn't the sort of boy who could forgive a younger brother who was better and brighter in every way than himself. If I'd shown you any favouritism it would have only made his resentment worse. I might have gone overboard,' Edgar conceded gruffly, 'but you were never a team player,' he accused. 'Always so damned headstrong, you never gave an inch. I exerted a lot of pressure to keep you at that damned school, called in several favours, offered to build them a new library. All you had to do was say you were sorry—not a lot to ask considering the fact you were responsible for two dislocations, one fracture and several missing teeth!'

'I didn't emerge exactly unscathed.'

'Would you apologise? You wouldn't budge an inch! You've never needed anyone,' Edgar accused harshly.

Tess watched as the heavy eyelids drooped protectively over Rafe's eyes. Her heart bled for him. When the extravagant sweep of dark lashes lifted there was absolutely no expression in those dark, shining depths.

'I don't need you,' he told his father with cold deliberation.

Tess found she actually felt sorry for the proud old man. She looked at his lined face; for the first time it was obvious that he really was old—old and tired.

'Why now?' Rafe asked.

'I could die and you wouldn't know… I couldn't let that responsibility fall on your mother. It suddenly seemed important for you to know.'

The pager vibrated in Tess's pocket. Torn by her conflicting desire to be in two places at once, she placed her hand on Rafe's arm and spoke his name. He looked at the small hand and then her face with an expression that suggested he'd forgotten she was there.

'I've got to go.'

'I'm coming with you.'

'But...' One look in his eyes made her bite back her response.

'We should be able to transfer him to the ward in the morning.'

'I'm so grateful,' Tess said for the hundredth time. She was, though. She was pathetically grateful for the people whose skill had saved Ben's life.

'You'll be welcome to stay on the ward with him, but he isn't going to wake up here until we reduce the sedation. What you should do is go home and get some sleep.'

'I couldn't possibly—' she began.

'I'll see she does, Doctor,' Rafe interrupted her.

Tess looked up at him indignantly as the doctor responded to a fresh call on his attention. 'I'm staying.'

'So that you're falling asleep tomorrow and the next day when Ben actually does need you?' When it was put like that, she was forced to concede that her all-night vigil didn't look like a practical solution. 'It's up to you, I suppose, but...'

'All right, all right,' she conceded crossly, casting one last look at the small sleeping figure. 'But they'll call me if...'

'Haven't they said they would, ad infinitum?' He sighed. 'Come on, Tess, you're only getting in the way,' he told her brutally.

'Thanks a lot!' Deep down she knew what Rafe was saying made sense, but she resented hearing him say it all the same.

'I'll take you home.'

She nodded reluctantly.

Tess inserted her door key into the lock and discovered that in her haste she'd left the door ajar. 'Are you coming in?'

she asked tentatively, turning to the tall figure standing just behind her.

'That was the general idea, but if you've got any objections...?'

The moon was bright but the flagstoned path was overhung with a thick canopy of heavy branches and his face remained a slightly paler shadow amongst many shadows.

'After what you've done for Ben, you think I'm going to slam the door in your face?'

'I was sort of hoping your welcome might be motivated by something other than gratitude.'

Flustered by his unfriendly tone, Tess pushed her fringe off her forehead. 'I didn't mean...of course I want you...that is, I don't *want* you.' Liar, liar... 'I want you to come in.'

He waited with apparent patience for her to finish tying herself into knots and subside into embarrassed silence. 'If you're worried I'll try slaking my lust at an inopportune moment, I'll take the couch.'

Despite the debilitating exhaustion invading just about every cell of her body, the prospect of lust-slaking didn't sound so awfully bad to Tess.

'Actually,' she told him, blinking against the harsh electric light in the narrow hallway, 'I thought it might be nice to hold someone and be held.' She didn't much care if she sounded forward and pushy, she didn't want to be alone.

'*Just someone?*'

Tess gave an exasperated sigh. 'No, not just someone...just you, actually. Happy now?' What a silly question—of course he wasn't happy! 'Do you want to talk about—?' she offered gently.

'No!' he cut in savagely. 'I don't want to talk to or about my grandfather...sorry, *father*.' Tess winced at the palpable bitterness in his voice. 'I suppose this makes my father my half-brother...?' He gave a bitter laugh. 'Talk about happy families.'

She knew he should talk; she knew he had to talk—she was equally sure that now wasn't the time for her to point it out. Taking his big hand in hers, she led him upstairs to her bed.

Tess slept straight away. She wasn't sure if Rafe did; she suspected not. When she woke some time later it was still dark and she could tell from the light shallowness of his breathing that Rafe was awake too. In the shadows she could see his back was turned to her. She'd fallen asleep in his arms—it didn't feel right not to wake up in the same place.

She felt the quiver run through his lean body when she placed her hand on his back, but he didn't move or protest when she leant across and started to massage the smooth flesh across his broad bare shoulders. She could feel the tight knots bunched under the silky surface. Tess was breathing hard from a combination of exertion and excitement by the time the tension had eased.

'Better?' she whispered softly, pulling herself closer until her front was hard against the strong curve of his back. His deep sigh was the sort of confirmation she'd hoped for.

She slid her arm over his shoulder and ran an exploratory hand down lower over his hard torso.

'What are you doing, Tess?'

'Touching you,' she told him, widening her area of interest. 'Do you mind?'

Suddenly the idea of payment for services rendered didn't seem so attractive. In fact it left a very sour taste in his mouth. He wanted her to do this because she needed to—needed to as badly as he did.

'You don't have to do this because you feel you have to repay me.'

Tess wished she could see his face. 'Is that a polite way of saying you're not in the mood?'

'I only want you to do this if—'

Her voice, high and unsteady, cut across his. 'If I can't think of anything else but the taste and smell and feel of you. I can't think about anything but having you kiss and touch me…feeling you move inside me.' A wild little laugh bubbled up inside her. 'Is that enough wanting for you, Rafe?'

She felt the growl vibrate deep down in his chest as, with a breathless display of speed, he turned over and pulled her on top of him.

'It'll do for now,' he confirmed, his dark eyes moving hungrily over the pale image of her face. 'It'll do just fine!'

He kissed her like a man starving for the taste of her lips. Tess responded with wild enthusiasm and deep relief. For one awful minute she'd thought he didn't want her. Rafe was a man whose life was being turned upside down. He was seeking an outlet for his frustration and she was more than willing to provide it. She pushed aside the depressing thought that his present need was only transitory.

CHAPTER EIGHT

TESS heard the taxi arrive just as Rafe, his sleeveless tee shirt wet with sweat, entered the kitchen. Breathing hard, he bent forward and braced his hands against his muscular thighs. His legs were dusted with a fine mesh of dark hair. Like his skin, they were dampened and glistened faintly. She swallowed and averted her gaze.

'I've been for a run,' he explained somewhat unnecessarily as he straightened up.

'So I see.' She checked she had put her mobile in her bag before snapping it shut and swinging it businesslike over one shoulder.

Her insides were mush and she felt about as businesslike as a limp stick of celery. She was driven to cast a furtive fleeting glance in his direction and instantly regretted it as, heart thudding painfully, she immediately withdrew her glance. How could you know someone for so long and not notice how simply *magnificent* they were?

'It helps me think.'

Tess nodded vaguely; she'd given up on sensible thought about five heartbeats earlier.

'I tried not to disturb you.'

Tess found herself praying he'd never appreciate the profound irony of that statement.

'About last night…' he began.

'Not now, Rafe, I need to get to the hospital.' To avoid looking at him, she opened her bag and pretended to be searching for something significant. She didn't want to hear him say that last night had been a mistake…not now—not ever, actually—but she was trying with limited success to be realistic.

131

Waking up alone had been enough realism to last her for the rest of the morning! She gritted her teeth against the deluge of loneliness that engulfed her when she recalled reaching sleepily out towards him only to find an empty pillow beside her.

'My taxi's waiting.'

'I can take you,' he said, peeling off his sweaty top in one elegant motion.

Tess took one look at his bronzed rippling torso and almost ran from the room. 'No, it's fine, the taxi's here,' she babbled before she put as much distance between her and Rafe as humanly possible.

Ben had already been transferred to the brightly decorated children's ward by the time she arrived. Chloe, one bruised side of her face an interesting multi-coloured rainbow of colours, sat beside him. She looked up when Tess walked in and got to her feet.

'How is he?' Tess asked, her eyes on the tiny, vulnerable figure in the bed.

'Doing even better than they expected.'

Tess gave a sigh of relief. 'They don't tell you a thing on the phone, do they? Don't get up on my account,' she said, feeling awkward. Who am I to come between mother and son...?

'No, I was just going to join Ian for a coffee. Tess...?'

'What, no aunty—?'

Chloe gave a sheepish smile. 'You're not actually much older than me, are you?' she said as if realising it for the first time. 'Could we talk a little later?' she asked, displaying a surprising amount of diffidence.

'Sure,' Tess agreed, trying not to sound as worried about the prospect as she felt.

It was Ian who came along a little later and suggested that she meet Chloe in the coffee shop while he sat with Ben. She didn't really have any legitimate excuse not to co-operate as Ben was dozing again, so reluctantly Tess agreed.

Ian touched her on the shoulder as she got to her feet. 'I know…' An impatient expression flickered across his handsome face. 'Who am I kidding? I don't begin to know how you must have felt when Chloe said she wanted to take the boy away.' His hand tightened on her shoulder. 'But I've got an imagination.' His eyes were warmly compassionate.

'I have to support Chloe in what she decides to do. Whatever that is,' he explained half apologetically. 'For what it's worth, I don't think she thought it through, and if it's any comfort,' he added thoughtfully, 'I think she's beginning to realise that too.'

Tess looked up at him and smiled. 'You really love her, don't you?'

Ian shrugged. 'For better, as they say, or worse.'

Impulsively Tess reached up and kissed him swiftly. 'I think Chloe is a very lucky girl,' she said huskily. She turned and almost walked slap bang into Rafe.

'What are you doing?'

He didn't reply immediately, just continued to glower furiously down at her, apparently in the grip of strong but dumb emotions.

'I'd ask you the same thing,' he replied eventually with a distinct lack of originality, 'if it wasn't so obvious.' He cast a particularly vicious glare towards Ian's back. Tess could almost visualise the daggers protruding from between the older man's shoulder blades.

I'll be damned if I'm going to apologise for an innocent peck on the cheek, she decided, lifting her chin defiantly.

'I'm going to see Chloe,' she explained, waiting impatiently for him to move. He didn't.

'I thought they were discharging her this morning. Has she had a relapse?' He didn't sound too devastated by the prospect.

'No, she hasn't, I'm meeting her in the coffee shop.' At last he moved to one side but, unfortunately from her point of view—she couldn't think straight with him around—he fell into step beside her. *'Alone,'* she added pointedly. Experience told her there was very little point being subtle with Rafe.

'Are you trying to tell me I'm not wanted?'

'I think Chloe might find your disapproving presence intimidating.'

'And do I intimidate you?' The idea seemed to startle and intrigue him.

'You irritate me.'

'It's mutual,' he came back immediately. 'I expect Chloe might be irritated herself if she knew you'd been kissing her boyfriend,' he sneered nastily.

His bizarre dog-in-the-manger behaviour flabbergasted Tess. 'Are you going to tell her?'

Rafe's dissatisfied sneer deepened.

'Have you any idea how silly you sound, not to mention look?' she wondered.

Rafe looked struck by her barbed comment. Twin bands of dark colour stained the sharp angle of his cheekbones as he mentally reviewed his behaviour. 'And whose fault is that?' he complained testily.

'I take it I'm meant to throw up my hands in culpability at this point.'

'You can do what you like with your hands, although I could put forward some interesting suggestions,' he mumbled in a dark velvety undertone that made Tess's insides melt, 'so long as you keep them off that actor guy!'

His sentiment was so unexpected and so belligerently unreasonable that Tess momentarily lost her powers of speech completely. When they returned she was sizzling mad.

'If I want to grope the entire county cricket side I won't ask your permission!' she announced somewhat ambitiously.

'Since when did you know how many were in a cricket team?'

She tossed her head. 'The more the merrier, as far as I'm concerned.' It occurred to Tess that for someone who had not so long ago accused Rafe of sounding silly she wasn't doing so bad herself! 'Why don't you go away?'

'You want me to?'

The question stopped Tess in her tracks; her righteous indignation fizzled away. 'Not really,' she conceded huskily. It had been bad enough waking without him this morning—the idea of Rafe vanishing off her personal horizon left her experiencing profound panic. Maybe she was only delaying the inevitable, but for the moment that didn't matter. To her relief Rafe didn't milk her admission—it was probably worth several pints of humiliation. He appeared happy to accept her reply at face value.

'If you feel the need to kiss men, I'm available.'

A small superior smile curved her lips as she raised her face to him. 'You call that a kiss,' she mocked.

'No, I call *this* a kiss.' He proceeded to demonstrate the difference. Rafe's persuasive powers were quite remarkable.

'Yes…well…' Tess remarked vaguely when her head stopped spinning. 'That was…' his politely quizzical expression invited her to elaborate on the theme '…completely unnecessary,' she announced severely.

His dark eyes crinkled deliciously around the edges as his expression got all intimate and personal. 'But quite nice?'

Tess cleared her throat. '*Very* nice, actually, but I still don't want you to come with me.'

Rafe seemed prepared to accept her decision this time. 'Fair enough,' he drawled, giving a good impression of a reasonable, fair-minded individual he wasn't! 'I'll see you later.'

'You will?' Tess frowned. The words had emerged far too breathlessly hopeful for her peace of mind.

'I'll be around,' he assured her, heading off in the opposite direction with a casual farewell salute.

For how long? she brooded, trying to turn her thoughts to Chloe and what she might want to say. It turned out Chloe said a lot and almost all of it surprised Tess.

'Children, they're a big responsibility, aren't they?' Chloe fretfully toyed with the bracelet around her slender wrist.

'It was an accident, you can't blame yourself,' Tess soothed.

'I don't,' Chloe responded immediately, looking puzzled. 'I suppose you've felt like this every time he's been ill. I couldn't bear it!' she choked.

'I try not to be overprotective, but it's an uphill battle,' Tess admitted. 'There are compensations, you know,' she added quietly. 'Children give a lot more than they take.'

Chloe looked unconvinced. 'I…I'm not used to worrying about anyone but myself,' she confessed in a rush.

Tess hadn't thought Chloe was capable of such self-awareness. She felt quite dismayed by the maturity it implied—maturity she'd always been happy to believe Chloe lacked. Perhaps she could make a good mother, given support and an opportunity. She forced herself to consider the unpalatable possibility that she wasn't the best person to take care of Ben—not if he had a real mother with a loving partner ready and willing to take on the role.

'That's perfectly normal. Neither was I before I started taking care of Ben.'

'That's not true, you were always taking care of some stray or other,' Chloe interrupted with an impatient gesture. 'I'm selfish, and I *like* being selfish.' She threw out the words like a challenge and waited for Tess to supply the condemnation; when she didn't Chloe's expression grew frustrated.

'I know you think it's pathetic, but I like being the one everyone fusses and worries about. I don't like sharing Ian with anyone.' She bit her lip and lowered her eyes. Tess had to strain to hear what she said. 'Ben called for you after the accident. Ian told me.'

'Well, he hardly knows you…' Tess swallowed and silently cursed the overdeveloped scruples that wouldn't permit her to take advantage of the situation '...*yet*,' she added, softening the blow.

'Why are you doing this?' Chloe wondered, lifting her head jerkily. Her eyelashes, for once undarkened, were wet. 'You don't want me to take Ben away. All you had to do was tell me what an inadequate, awful excuse for a mother I am, and we both know it would be true. Why are you being kind to me?' Unwittingly she echoed the question Tess was asking herself.

'You are Ben's mother.'

'I gave birth to him.'

'What exactly are you saying, Chloe?'

'I'm saying he should stay with you.'

Tess didn't know she'd been carrying around the leaden weight until it magically lifted off her slender shoulders. 'For how long?' she asked when caution and common sense overcame relief. She wasn't sure if she could go through all this in another few years when Chloe once more changed her mind.

'Permanently. We'll make it legal, if you like.'

'Are you sure? Perhaps you should wait.'

'I've made up my mind. There isn't any room in my life for children, not for years and years... Maybe not ever.'

'How does Ian feel about that?' Tess wondered.

Chloe looked surprised by the question. 'Ian wants me to be happy,' she explained simply.

The student nurse permitted herself a second backward glance as she moved away from the tall figure who was now bending solicitously over the child sleeping in the cot. She wondered if it would be unprofessional to ask for his autograph.

Tess's eyes narrowed cynically as she noted the backward glance. 'Did she call you...?'

'*Daddy?* Yes, she did,' Rafe admitted, looking a little startled by the experience. 'That's a first.'

Probably not a last, though, Tess reflected, nibbling at her neatly trimmed fingernails. Rafe could produce as many babies as he wanted in the future.

'I feel I should be wearing slippers…a pipe might be pushing it…' he conceded.

'If it's any comfort, I don't think little Miss Nightingale was regarding you in the cosy dependable light.'

'*Really!*' He made a point of looking around hopefully for the trim white-clad figure. The acid in Tess's glare increased tenfold and he grinned widely. 'You haven't done that for years,' he observed, taking the spare chair beside the sleeping boy's bed.

Tess snatched her hand self-consciously from her mouth. 'It's been a stressful day.'

Rafe's deep sigh suggested he agreed with her. 'He's asleep, then.'

He made it sound as though this peaceful state of affairs had been achieved without a great deal of patience and persuasion.

'Small thanks to you.'

'You asked me to amuse him,' Rafe protested.

'Save that hurt, bemused look for the nursing staff!' she advised tartly, allowing her glare to include the slim figure in an attractive uniform who was once more drifting past. 'I've already had to suffer gushing reports of how much nicer and better-looking you are in the flesh.'

Her eyes moved of their own accord to the small V of olive-toned flesh revealed by the neckline of the knitted polo shirt he was wearing. Don't think flesh—don't think flesh, she instructed herself firmly.

'She's back again,' she muttered in a tight-lipped undertone. 'Call me a cynic, but are we getting more attention now you're back?'

'You're a cynic,' he repeated obligingly. 'Is it my fault I have fatal charm?'

Tess snorted. It was less easy to treat his lethal charm

lightly when you'd fallen victim to it as irrevocably as she had. 'I asked you to amuse Ben. If I'd known you were going to overstimulate him I wouldn't have bothered taking a break.'

'You wouldn't have bothered eating either.' He subjected her slim figure to a thoughtful, narrow-eyed inspection. 'And you can't afford to lose any weight.'

Tess's sense of misuse increased. 'I didn't notice you being so picky last night.'

'I'm always picky, Tess,' he assured her soothingly.

The way he was looking at her made her heart beat wildly against its confinement in her chest. She swallowed. 'You've no idea how flattered I feel,' she drawled sarcastically.

'You've no idea what sort of personal interest I take in how you feel,' he came back smoothly.

Tess decided a swift change of subject would be a good idea. 'He was pumped up so high I thought he was going to self-combust,' she grumbled. The student nurse bustled by yet again and Tess's expression grew pained. 'Why didn't you tell her you're not?' she demanded in a pained whisper.

'Not what? Irresistible…available…?'

'Ben's dad. She already thinks I'm his mum. If she thinks you're his father she'll think…think we're…' Under his interested innocent gaze, the colour bloomed darkly in her cheeks.

'Intimate…?' His voice was a seductive rasp that made all the fine hairs on her nape dance. He folded his arms and settled further back in his seat, smiling with malicious pleasure at her hot cheeks. 'Having carnal relations? Doing *it*…? What a *shocking* thought!'

'Must you be crude and vulgar?' she choked.

'Must you worry about what people think?' he came back with equal distaste. 'Besides, I would have thought that you of all people would have appreciated that it's easier not to say anything sometimes. People in glass houses, my pet…'

'I'm not your pet!' she snapped, her eyes flashing green fire.

His eyes dropped to her heaving bosom. 'No,' he agreed softly. 'More feral than domesticated…but definitely feline.'

'Will you stop talking nonsense?'

'Yes, it probably is about time we got serious.'

She didn't like the sound of that at all. 'It is?'

'We can't talk here.' He gave a dissatisfied grimace as he looked around the quiet, dimly lit ward. 'Let's go somewhere more private. I've been trying to talk to you all day, only you keep running away.'

And if there were anywhere left to run she'd still be doing so. 'I don't want to go anywhere private with you, so will you kindly stop manhandling me?' she hissed. 'You're making us conspicuous.'

'I think gentle encouragement is nearer the mark, but have it your own way.' Ostentatiously Rafe removed his hand from her shoulder. 'Anyone would think I'd flung you caveman-style over my shoulder—a method, incidentally, I don't see much wrong with.'

'That comes as no surprise to me, but I can think of a few other people to whom it might. If only those dynamic lady politicians you have eating out of your hand could hear their charming, politically correct host now!'

'Is that a threat?' he asked, not sounding particularly bothered.

'Depends on how far you push me,' she grumbled.

'I'm prepared to push you the whole way if that's what it takes,' he explained cryptically with a pleasant and spine-chillingly ruthless smile. 'However, for the present this ought to be far enough. Good, it's empty,' he announced briskly, after poking his head around the door of the small sitting room reserved for parents. 'In my capacity as your lover—you'll probably say I was exceeding my authority.' It was hard to miss the fact he didn't actually look or sound particularly apologetic.

This was a description that she couldn't let pass. 'Your capacity as *what*?' It was the wrong time for a stab of sexual hunger to tie her stomach in knots.

'You prefer boyfriend?' He appeared to give frowning consideration to the option. 'A bit tepid, don't you think? Anyhow, leaving my official title to one side for the moment, I refused entry to a visitor for Ben earlier.' He looked as if the memory afforded him a considerable degree of pleasure.

'Who?' she managed weakly.

'My grand… Sorry about that.' His lips formed a humourless parody of a smile. 'My father.'

That explained the pleasure part.

'And he went away…just like that?' That didn't sound like the Edgar Farrar she knew.

'Not just like that exactly—you could say he needed a bit of convincing. He queried my right to eject him, too.'

Tess was striving for philosophical but it wasn't easy. 'But you managed to convince him.'

'I just explained how things were,' he announced airily.

'Perhaps when you've got a moment or two you might do the same for me…only not now!' she begged drily when he opened his mouth to oblige. 'There's a limit to the number of shocks my nervous system can take in one twenty-four-hour period. Did you get around to asking what he wanted?'

'Ben, I should think…wouldn't you?' Rafe watched the colour retreat, leaving her marble pale. The hand she raised to her lips was visibly shaking.

'You're not serious.'

'Forget me,' he advised. 'It's the old man you have to worry about and he's deadly serious. Ben's his grandson and, as far as he's concerned, a Farrar. He's taken one Farrar from his mother,' Rafe reminded her grimly. 'You don't honestly think he'd have any scruples about doing it again?

Sit down,' he said softly, pushing her down into one of the soft easy chairs.

'But Chloe is Ben's mother and she wants me...'

'Will Chloe remain resolute if Edgar waves a dirty great cheque in front of her sensitive nose?' He waved an invisible bribe before her nose and, on the point of removing his hand, seemed to have second thoughts. 'You've got a kind of cute nose.' He allowed the tip of his thumb to gently graze the tip of her small neat nose. The action had all the hallmarks of compulsion about it. 'Has anyone ever told you that?' His voice carried a degree of intensity that didn't match the joking frivolity of the comment.

'That's a horrible thing to imply.'

'That you've got a cute nose?' Despite her defence of her niece, Rafe could clearly see the doubt in her troubled emerald eyes. He withdrew his hand but let his fingers slide down the curve of her cheek as he did so; he felt the vibration of the quiver that involved her entire body. He was glad about that quiver; if a man was going to get obsessional about possessing a woman's body, it made it less worrying if she felt the same way.

Tess pulled her eyes from the dark, mesmeric hold of his unblinking regard. I am, she decided forlornly, addicted to the man.

'You know what I mean,' she protested huskily.

And I know what you're feeling. 'Don't shoot me, angel. I'm only the messenger.'

'You could try not to look as though you enjoy your work.'

'It might be different if you were married and financially solvent. The old man would find it hard to prove you're not a fit person to care for Ben then.'

'Would he take things that far?' she asked dubiously.

'You could wait and find out, or you could take pre-emptive action.'

'I'm not a military unit!'

'You might be a military target, though. You forget Edgar was the younger son before his big brother took a bullet in the war. All younger male Farrars do their obligatory stint…officers and gentlemen, one and all…' He gave a mock salute.

'Except you.'

'Except me,' he conceded. 'The old man is particularly fond of pointing out that I'm not gentleman material. He's also fond of saying that his military background always gives him the edge over competitors. Nothing like honing a man's natural homicidal tendencies to equip him for life in the financial jungle.'

When it came to survival techniques Tess doubted there was anything anyone could teach Rafe—mind you, he would have made a uniform look as good as humanly possible.

'Anyone would be excused for thinking you're trying to panic me. I'm a respectable, responsible person.'

'A pillar of the community,' he agreed obligingly.

'And I'm *not* in debt,' she gritted.

'Maybe not, but you don't have much put aside for the odd rainy day.'

Tess chewed her lips as she silently acknowledged the truth of what he was saying. 'There are more important things than money.'

'Not when you haven't got any.'

Tess gritted her teeth. Why was it Rafe *always* had an answer? 'Ben's older now, and I'll be able to go back to work soon.'

'A latchkey kid—that should go down well.'

'I was talking about a nanny, not neglect!'

'There is a simple solution…'

'Sure, I could win the lottery. *Well…?*' she prompted when his dramatic pause got too lengthy for her impatience. 'I'm a captive audience—what are you waiting for?'

'Marry me.'

Tess's eyes widened to their fullest extent and a tiny choking sound emerged from her parted lips as she shook her head.

'Strange—you don't look mad.' Then again, he didn't look like a man proposing either.

There was a distinct lack of tender emotion in his hard, unflinching gaze. He looked more like a man determined to push through a particularly unpopular business deal against all the odds—maybe that wasn't such a bad analogy… Tess didn't think for one minute he actually wanted to marry her. He just wanted it *more* than he wanted Edgar to have any control over Ben's future.

'You'll laugh about this,' she continued, stifling a strong urge to weep loud and long, 'but for a minute there I thought you said—'

'I did.' There was a definite note of impatience in his voice. 'Marry me, Tess.'

'I knew I was imagining it, because not even you could come up with such a crazy idea.' Tess managed a slightly shaky laugh to demonstrate how amusing she found the entire notion.

'Why is it crazy?' There was a note of belligerence in his deep tone.

'Listen, even if there was a possibility of your…of Edgar trying to get custody of Ben—which I don't think for one minute is going to happen—there's no way I would even consider marrying you.'

'You're sleeping with me.'

To her intense frustration and growing desperation, he showed no signs of having heard her at all—the man had the flexibility of a steel bar! She decided to appeal to the rational side of his nature.

'There's a big difference between casually sleeping with someone and marrying them, Rafe.'

Rafe clenched his even white teeth until she heard them grind—it wasn't the most *rational* sound she'd ever heard.

'Meaning any convenient body would have done as well as mine!'

'Of course not!' she responded indignantly. 'I couldn't possibly sleep with anyone else but you!' she told him in a voice that throbbed with conviction.

Any male could be forgiven for looking slightly complacent when a woman made that sort of announcement—Tess suspected her candour was going to cost her dear this time.

Rafe visibly relaxed. If he didn't actually preen himself, he came remarkably close. 'Then that's a good start.'

'I meant that...' Go on, Tess, what did you mean? 'I'd have to stop sleeping with you before I...I...' Until she'd actually put it into words, Tess hadn't really given much thought to how hard the transition back to a less intimate relationship was going to be. The prospect was one of the most depressing scenarios she'd ever contemplated.

'Move on to pastures new?' he suggested delicately when her hoarse voice dried up completely. 'I think on the whole that's probably wise. It can be hell trying to keep too many balls up in the air at once.'

'You'd know, I suppose,' she choked.

'I thought I'd already established that I'm strictly a monogamous sort of guy.'

Tess gave a soft moan of pure exasperation and tried to formulate a single sentence that would put paid for good to his flights of fancy. All she managed to come up with was rather weak and tremulous.

'You know I can't get married.'

He shook his head and ruthlessly pushed aside her objection. 'I *know* you can't have my children.'

It was true, but it hurt to hear him say it all the same. 'It amounts to the same thing.'

'Ben would be our family.'

There was something awfully seductive about his logic and his air of complete certainty.

'Stop trying to hustle me, Farrar,' she growled. 'I know

you want to thumb your nose at Edgar, but isn't this going a bit far?'

Rafe didn't deny her accusation, but then he wouldn't because basically he was a decent, honest man. If he weren't he would have been telling her the sort of things she wanted to hear—things such as he loved her—but he hadn't.

'It was only a little while ago you were going to marry someone else.'

'That was entirely different.'

Of course it was; he'd loved her—still did. 'Yes, *I'm* not already married.'

'That really bothers you, doesn't it?'

Tess bristled, resenting the implication her attitude was prudish. 'Call me a freak—'

'I wouldn't do that—'

She loftily ignored his interruption, and found it harder to ignore the warmth in his eyes. The starch went out of her spine and she sighed.

'Yes, as a matter of fact it does bother me. I happen to think that if you make vows you should stick by them. If you don't...'

'If you don't, things like me happen.' He met her confused look with a thin-lipped sardonic smile. 'If it hadn't been for marital infidelity I wouldn't be here...but maybe you don't think that would be a great loss?' he teased. 'I won't cheat, if that's what is bothering you, Tess, and I know ignorance is no defence in law, but I was sort of hoping you'd be a little more flexible? I honestly didn't know Claudine was married when we met and when I did find out she swore to me her marriage was over in all but name.'

She'd sworn a lot of things that had turned out not to be true—things such as she wasn't sleeping with her husband, she still loved Rafe, she just loved her husband as well, or, as it had turned out, *more*—and he'd believed them all because he'd wanted to believe them. He'd wanted to be needed, not just for his looks or his money, but needed for himself. It had finally got to the point where self-deception hadn't worked any more.

'And it wasn't?' Tess persisted masochistically. Nothing showed in his eyes but she had the impression a lot was going on behind that enigmatic façade.

'She's pregnant and it's not mine. Does that answer your question?'

'Are you sure?' she blurted out without thinking.

'My dear Tess, do you think I'd have had unprotected sex with you if there was the *remotest* possibility I could have passed anything to you?' he asked her incredulously. 'The baby is *definitely* not mine.'

'Are you saying you've never *not* used…with anyone else…*ever*…?' She'd been more articulate in her life but it seemed Rafe hadn't had much problem following her.

'A first for us both, angel.'

She drew a shaky sigh. 'I suppose it was because you knew I couldn't get pregnant.'

'I wasn't thinking of consequences at the time…*were you*?'

Tess's stomach muscles spasmed. She tore her eyes from his dark intense gaze and fixed them on her hands, which lay white-knuckled and tightly intertwined in her lap. How could she forget that primal need to surrender, to be possessed, when she felt the same way, give or take the odd ache every time she looked at him? Hell, look nothing—every time she *thought* about him!

'I met Claudine when her marriage was going through a rough patch,' she heard him recall. 'She admitted to me at the end that the only reason she slept with me originally was to pay her husband back for an indiscretion.'

Tess winced. 'Not good for the ego, I grant you, but that's a position a lot of men must fantasise about finding themselves in.' Contemplating the shallow nature of the male of the species, she gave a cynical smile and flexed her stiff fingers to encourage the circulation to return. 'Especially if the vengeful wife happens to be drop-dead gorgeous, of course.'

She wasn't shocked when he didn't jump in and explain that Claudine had been nothing to look at—since when did men make fools of themselves over a sweet nature?

'It just so happens that I'm not one of them…or,' Rafe conceded with a shrug, 'not on this occasion, I wasn't. Ironically, when she told the husband about me it seemed it revived his interest. I must have put the spark back in their sex life—quite a feather in my cap, don't you think?'

Under the circumstances Tess wasn't surprised that there was an air of suppressed violence about him. The husband's interest had resulted in a baby, without which Rafe might be with Claudine at this very moment…?

'Hard luck.'

Some of her feelings must have shown in her voice because he looked up, the bitter, distracted expression gradually fading from his face.

'How did we come to be talking about that?'

'Let's see,' she mused, pressing a finger to the tiny suggestion of a cleft in her rounded chin. 'You asked me to marry you, then to clinch the deal you started pointing out the plus points of marital infidelity, and for good measure finished off going into painful details about your ill-fated love for the much-married and embarrassingly fertile Claudine.'

'Hell, Tess, you make it sound—'

'Boring?'

A thoughtful frown creased his forehead. 'You don't sound bored.'

He was too sharp for his own good—or hers!

'I'm polite.'

He permitted himself a wry grin at this assertion. 'I'll let that one pass.' His expression sobered. 'You sound angry.'

'Would it be so unreasonable if I was? You were mad when you caught me innocently kissing Ian. You don't have to be in love with someone not to like the idea of them slobbering over someone else!' she finished shrilly.

'I didn't say you were in love with me.'

Panic raced through her tense body. No, he didn't, but if I don't keep my stupid tongue still the whole world and his neighbour will know. It was too late now to retract her words—she'd just have to tough it out.

'Of course you didn't. You're stupid and vain, but not *that* stupid and vain.' She saw there was still shadowy suspicion in his eyes and her bolshiness faded; it wasn't getting her anywhere. When she managed to compose herself there was the unmistakable ring of authenticity to her words. 'If you must know, the idea of you touching me while you're thinking of...' She broke off and covered her mouth with a trembling hand. 'It makes me feel ill,' she revealed in a tearful whisper.

Rafe swore and dropped down on his knees before her. There were some things which everyone but a totally insensitive fool would realise! One of them was that there were some things you could discuss openly with your best friend that you couldn't discuss if she unexpectedly became your lover. Top of that list was other women.

Did this mean that the price of intimacy would be a loss of the closeness they'd always enjoyed? He'd no longer enjoy the freedom to say exactly what he felt around her? He hoped not.

'Of course it does, angel, only I wouldn't...I haven't.' He took her face between his hands and looked into her tear-filled eyes. The slight quiver of her soft pink lips drew his attention to the full passionate curve...actually his appetite never had run to sugary confections, and Tess was definitely more spice than sugar.

'I honestly can't think of anything or anyone but you when we're in bed together.'

A man would have to be crazy to admit his mind wandered while he was making love to a woman, especially if that wandering took him in the direction of another woman. It struck Rafe forcibly at that moment that he didn't need to seek refuge in prevarication—loving Tess had not left room for any intrusive thoughts. There had been nothing and nobody for him but Tess—his senses had been saturated with her. A flicker of confusion passed over his face before he continued.

'I fell in love with Claudine...' he heard the odd defensive note creep into his voice and his frown deepened '...but what did it get me? Nothing but a short stint in hell! I *never*,' he told her in a voice that came straight from the heart, 'want to feel like that again. No,' he explained to her warmly, 'what we have is much *much* better. We have incredible sex. Admittedly,' he conceded realistically, 'that might not last.' Experiencing a sudden flashback of her slender, sweat-slick body arched beneath him, Rafe determined to do everything within his power to keep their passion alive.

Now there, Tess thought bitterly, was a prospect to keep a girl warm at nights.

'But we'll still be friends; we'll *always* be friends. What could be a better basis for a lasting marriage? Sometimes the solution is so simple you don't notice it.'

So long as he doesn't have any more revelations! The longer he remained oblivious to things like the neon sign above her head saying, 'I love you, you idiot' in great big letters, the better!

Maybe he was having second thoughts. His enthusiasm sounded a bit forced to her—almost as forced as the smile she responded to his concern with.

'It's all right if you want to talk about Claudine,' she lied bravely. 'I was being silly.'

Her tolerant generosity seemed to go down like a lead balloon.

'I don't want to talk about her.'

Tess caught his hands as they fell from her face and gave them a comforting squeeze. 'I understand.'

'Lucky you.'

'I can also understand why you want things to be simple after what you've just been through, but don't you see if we get married things won't be simple any more? The way things stand you…either of us can just walk away at any time.'

'So you're willing to lose Ben to the old man just because you want to keep your options open in case a better prospect in bed happens along!' Rafe shook off her hands and she watched his own ball into fists.

Tess shook her head in disbelief. 'Only you could turn this around so that I'm the selfish one.'

Rafe pressed his face into his hands before lifting his head and dragging them through his dark hair. 'You're right.' His ready retraction did more to sap her resolve than all the moral blackmail in the world. 'I'm sorry, Tess. It's just I know what it's like to be brought up in a house where you feel nobody wants you. Together we could make sure that Ben knew he was wanted every day of his life.'

His conviction was deeply compelling. Tess found herself reaching out to touch the side of his face. His jaw was velvet-rough under her fingertips.

'That's a truly lovely thing to say, Rafe.'

He looked embarrassed. 'I mean it.'

'I believe you, Rafe, it's just…' She felt too emotional to continue.

'We can make it work. I *know* we can.'

'For Ben's sake?' It would make all the difference if she didn't already know the answer to that question.

His eyes slid from hers. 'You know me, Tess, I'm not big on self-sacrifice.'

'You're not trying to pretend you *want* to marry me!'

His broad shoulders lifted as he captured her small hands in his. 'Should I?'

She pursed her lips and grated her teeth in exasperation. 'You've started to pick up a lot of nasty habits from the political types you interview. You're getting as slippery as they are.'

'I don't know what you mean.' He was the picture of injured innocence.

Tess snorted. 'Don't come the innocent with me, Rafe. I'm not saying another thing to you if you continue to respond to everything I ask you with a question.'

'Was I that obvious?'

She nodded.

He shook his head. 'I must be slipping. You're *really* not going to say another word.' Another nod. 'You promise?' Rafe gave a slow, wolfish grin. 'In that case...' The long, curling eyelashes lifted and Tess watched transfixed as the sizzling desire stirred smokily in his spectacular eyes.

From where he knelt their heads were almost level. A long, soundless sigh emerged from her slightly parted lips just before Rafe threw his rigid control to the winds and took full advantage of her self-imposed silence.

Tess melted into his embrace and with a tiny lost whimper wrapped her slim arms around his neck. Weakened by a flood of scalding desire, she shamelessly clung onto him. There was blind urgency in the long, hungry kiss which went on and on until Tess thought she'd simply melt.

When his lips left hers they didn't go very far. His nose pressed against the side of hers, he stayed there breathing hard. Even the touch of his warm breath against her skin aroused her to the point of babbling delirium.

'I love—' she only stopped herself just in time '—the way you kiss.'

There was a slight uneven catch in his deep warm laugh. Her skin was moist where tiny pinpricks of moisture had exploded across the surface; she could feel that his skin was damp too. Without thinking of the consequences she dabbed her tongue against the salty sheen across his jaw. His splayed fingers were pressed against her back. They spasmed and for a moment the pressure was painful. The moment passed swiftly and the hand that continued to move up and down the length of her spine became almost soothing. It also effectively prevented her drawing back; as it happened the last thing on Tess's mind was escape.

'You've absolutely no idea how much I've been wanting to do that,' he groaned, taking her chin in one hand and pressing another urgent kiss to her soft, inviting lips. *'Last night...'* The muscles in his throat visibly worked as he swallowed hard. 'Oh, God, Tess, it was...' He gave a hoarse cry. This time his kiss was tender, lingering.

'We shouldn't be doing this...here.' Tess made a token protest even though she was exactly where she wanted to be.

'Doing what?' he asked indulgently as he brushed back her fringe to reveal a shapely broad forehead. 'Kissing?'

'I'm leaning on you.' She made it sound a shameful thing to be doing. Leaning seemed somehow more significant to her than kissing; it implied trust, dependence, reliance, vulnerability—things that Tess had no practice displaying.

What am I doing? The man hasn't just offered me his soul, just a marriage of convenience, she reminded herself brutally. It was crazy and dangerous to lower her defences and respond like this.

Rafe seemed to understand instinctively what she was saying... I suppose it's just as well one of us does! she thought.

'That's the idea, Tess, that's what I'm here for. You don't have to shoulder the responsibility alone any more.'

Oh, he'd like that, wouldn't he, if she got all meek and compliant? Tess tried to ignite the dregs of her resentment and failed miserably.

'You've told your grandfather we're getting married, haven't you?'

'I knew I couldn't pull the wool over your eyes.'

She dug her fingers deep in the thick hair that curled against his neck. 'But you thought you'd try anyway. I suppose the theory is that this makes it even harder for me to say no.'

An irrepressible grin split his lean features. 'I knew you wanted to say yes!'

Tess's eyes widened. It wasn't just his audacity and arrogance that drew an outraged gasp from her, it was his perception. Her fingers twisted tighter in his hair until he held up his hands in mock surrender.

'You...you manipulative...'

'You know me so well, angel.' There was no laughter in his eyes as they ran over her face. 'And I'd like you to get to know me even better. I want you to be able to forget where Tess ends and Rafe starts.'

The erotic rasp in his voice made her shiver as his hands moved to either side of her slender shoulders. The pressure he exerted drew her body upwards.

'I wish you weren't staying here tonight... It's all right, I know you have to,' he soothed as she opened her mouth to speak. At that moment a distant cry made her stiffen.

'It's Ben!' she cried, pulling away from him. She pulled a shaking hand firmly across her tender lips and tried to compose herself. 'I have to go.' She stated the obvious for his benefit as she leapt urgently to her feet.

For a moment he stayed where he was, on his knees. It seemed strange to see Rafe of all people in the position of a supplicant. Rafe didn't plead—he might go as far as to coax, cajole and generally confuse the issue, but not beg.

'How do you know?' He frowned. 'Know that it's Ben?'

Tess looked at him as though he'd just said something extremely stupid. She'd know Ben's cry if you hid it amongst another hundred others.

'I just *know*,' she announced impatiently.

Rafe reached the boy's bedside about the same time as the nurse. Tess was already soothing the fretful child.

CHAPTER NINE

TESS felt miserable that they'd argued before he'd left for town. She knew it was unreasonable to feel mad with Rafe for leaving in the middle of a sizzling row, but she did anyhow.

Nursing her rancour, she chose not to dwell on the fact he hadn't had much choice in the matter. It was quite a coup to get an interview with the latest high-profile political casualty. The higher they'd climbed, the more spectacular the fall and the greater the public interest—so far this chap had refused to speak to anyone but Rafe.

She couldn't even legitimately complain that Rafe put work ahead of everything else. He'd taken loads of time out of a crammed schedule when Ben had been in hospital and newly returned home.

He must be wondering what he had to do to make her happy...pity she couldn't tell him! The thing was, her emotions were all over the place. The emotional see-saw of dramatic mood swings was exhausting, which probably accounted for the intense, bone-deep fatigue she'd been experiencing lately.

She wasn't the only who looked less than bright-eyed and bushy-tailed. Rafe was displaying signs of strain too, but it was probably pretty tiring living with someone when you were never very sure if they were about to burst out crying or demand urgently to be made love to!

She gained some comfort from the fact Rafe always seemed happy to oblige her where the love-making was concerned—their communication problems didn't extend as far as the bedroom, where things remained several degrees better than blissful!

That initial anger she'd felt was now tinged by a steadily growing conviction that she might have overreacted slightly when she'd found out he'd put the announcement of their impending marriage in *The Times*.

Rafe's casual response when she'd waved the offending item under his eyes had transformed her shock into simmering anger.

'I meant to tell you, it must have slipped my mind.' Rafe slid the last item into his holdall. 'The old man might actually believe we're serious now,' he added, fastening the bag and heaving it over his shoulder.

His explanation didn't fool her; *nothing* slipped Rafe's mind!

'Edgar isn't the only one who will see it.'

Rafe's eyes narrowed suspiciously. 'And that bothers you?'

'It bothers me that people will expect me to act like a blushing bride,' she snapped.

It bothered her that she couldn't tell him she loved him. Part of her wanted to take the risk; she'd been on the point of blurting it out a hundred times. Sometimes she literally ached from wanting to tell him. If he'd ever given a single hint that he wanted anything more from her than sex, she might have.

'I can make you blush.' He used the soft intimate purr that acted on her like an instant aphrodisiac. His words reawakened the memory of the things he'd said to her when they'd made love that morning, things that had made her whole body burn.

Her stomach muscles contracted violently. Looking in his eyes felt like drowning…drowning in desire.

'God, I wish you didn't have to go!' she wailed hoarsely.

'Then come. Come with me,' he responded immediately.

A brilliant smile lit her face, then just as dramatically it faded. 'I can't—I'm not packed, neither is Ben. It isn't really practical.'

He shrugged as if it didn't matter to him anyway. 'But you're all right about the announcement?'

He didn't even care enough to try and persuade me... 'Does it matter?'

'A formal gesture might not be necessary if you were wearing my ring,' he drawled, his glance skimming her bare left hand.

Tess's hand curled into a tight fist. 'Not that again! I've told you...'

'That a ring is an outmoded symbol of ownership,' he recited in a monotonous monotone. 'Yes, you have, Tess—on numerous occasions, and if those were your genuine views I'd respect them, but we both know they're not.'

'You can't leave after saying something like that!' she cried, slamming the door he had just opened and leaning her back against it.

'Let's face it, Tess, you threw the ring back in my face because you're determined to act as if this marriage is some sort of cosmetic affair. A ring, an official announcement, it all makes it seem too real for your taste. When the vicar asks if you will, you'll probably say *maybe*!'

His accusation was so close to the mark she naturally got a lot madder.

'It may have escaped your notice, but this marriage *is* a cosmetic affair.' Her dulcet tone concealed desperate pain.

'This marriage,' he bit back, 'will be what we make of it. For Ben's sake...'

Does he think I'm likely to forget this is all for Ben's sake? she wondered miserably.

'We were talking about this,' she interrupted coldly, shaking the offending newspaper, 'yet another example of your high-handed behaviour and—' She stopped abruptly. 'Did you say vicar? I thought we'd agreed that a register office would be more appropriate?'

'I didn't agree with anything.' His gentle smile was provocative in the extreme as he opened the door with her still attached to it and calmly stepped through.

Her fury and frustration bubbling over, Tess followed him into the hallway, almost running to keep up with him as he made his way towards the front door of the cottage. Of all the stiff-necked, self-righteous, *stubborn*...

'You really are your father's son, aren't you?' she flung wildly at his broad-shouldered back.

That got his attention. He stopped and turned so abruptly that Tess had to dig her heels into the worn tread of the mellow-toned carpet that covered the oak boards to prevent herself catapulting into him.

'Did you just say that for effect, or have you actually got a point to make?'

Rafe had remarkably expressive eyes—had she been allowed she could have covered several sheets of A4 with adoring descriptions of those sensational velvety orbs—and right now they weren't saying anything flattering about Tess. A lesser soul, or possibly a less furious soul, than Tess might have been intimidated by the austere sneer that drew one corner of his mouth upwards at exactly the same fascinating angle as one quizzically haughty eyebrow.

'You're just as anxious to keep up appearances as Edgar is!' she told him, her lower lip quivering with disgust and disillusionment. 'I always thought you were more honest than that.'

If she'd thought for one second Rafe's extravagant plans had been inspired by anything other than a desire to make their marriage plans look authentic for the benefit of the world in general, and his father in particular, she'd have rejoiced and been more than happy to wear his ring. Hell, she'd have worn an elastic band if the reason he'd offered it had been that he loved her!

There had been no mention of love when he'd produced the ring; in fact his manner had been insultingly offhand. She would have happily been married in a cupboard, and by the same token would have walked down the aisle in a cathedral if the man who loved her wanted to shout about their love to the world! Knowing Rafe didn't just made her more reluctant to go along with his plans.

'I'm sorry if my integrity falls short of your standards.' The frigid silence lasted for a handful of seconds before he turned on his heel and left. Tess wanted to run after him, but she didn't.

During the miserable twenty-four hours since he'd been gone Tess had come to accept that she couldn't carry on punishing Rafe for not loving her. She ought to feel glad that at least when it came to important things he'd never pretended.

She was going into this marriage with her eyes open, it was Rafe who wasn't, which in her eyes made her the worst sort of hypocrite! The more she thought about it, the more convinced she became that she couldn't go through with the wedding without telling Rafe the truth, which was why she'd caught the train up to London and, with a holdall under one arm and a baby under the other, was now standing outside the building where Rafe lived.

Rafe's flat was on the top floor of the old warehouse conversion, a minimalist's paradise with acres of polished wood floors, lots of industrial chrome and light streaming in through vast windows that overlooked the river.

It made her feel even guiltier to recall that at a word from her he'd made it clear he was willing to sacrifice this bachelor haven for a more child-friendly environment. She wouldn't even wear his stupid ring!

Perhaps she'd feel better once she'd told him the truth. The flip side of that coin was that she could feel a lot worse if he reacted badly to the news his reluctant fiancée was actually wildly in love with him!

Tess opted for the lift. Stairs might be the healthier option, but not when you were carrying a sleepy toddler. Ben was making up for lost time—he seemed to have put on several pounds in the weeks since he'd been discharged from hospital.

I just hope that after all this Rafe's at home. Who are you kidding, Tess? she mocked herself. You're praying he won't be home. Just in case her prayers were answered and the inevitable was delayed, she'd brought the key he'd given her. Spontaneity was all well and good, but with a baby in tow it paid to make contingency plans.

As it happened she didn't need a key—the front door was ajar. Tess frowned. People—Rafe included—just didn't leave their doors open or even ajar in the security-conscious city. Either Rafe had had burglars or he'd been spending too much time in their crime-free village.

Not burglars, she decided, walking into the scrupulously tidy open-plan living area. The first thing that hit her was the absence of baby clutter. She pictured some blonde draped across the soft leather sofa and the bile rose in her throat. She'd never suspected that jealousy could be such a physical emotion. Along with the nausea, her throat was dry and her heart was palpitating as if she'd opted for stairs.

The anticlimax was tremendous when her call produced no response.

She wandered through to the bedroom, looking about her curiously. It had been a long time since she'd been here. The Japanese-style decor in the bedroom was new. With relief she knelt down and laid the sleeping child on the bed. Relieved of her burden, she flexed her aching shoulders.

Out of the corner of her eyes she caught a flicker of movement. It came from outside on the balcony that ran the length of the flat linking the living area to the master bedroom.

Don't think, just do it, she instructed herself firmly. The door slid silently across, and Tess was just about to step outside when she realised Rafe wasn't alone. She hastily drew back into the bedroom. Once she'd heard the voice was female there was no question of her closing the door and waiting.

'I knew when I saw the announcement in the paper what a terrible, *terrible* mistake I'd made, darling!' The unseen person pleaded in a breathy, little-girl whisper. 'You must know you're acting on the rebound. Don't do it, *please*!'

There was the sound of sobbing. It wasn't the sort of no-holds-barred sobbing that made a girl's eyes red and puffy; it was a delicate, restrained, eye-dabbing variety, designed to melt susceptible, protective male hearts.

Tess, her eyes closed tight, could visualise the sort of comfort going on during the nerve-racking silence. There was a scream building up somewhere in the tight confines of her chest.

'If it wasn't for the baby...we'd—'

Tess wondered how the other woman managed to make a laugh sound bitter and sexy simultaneously.

'I know it's not easy for any man to take on another man's child...'

'I might have agreed with you once. We live and learn.' There was a note of joyous discovery in Rafe's voice as he warmed to his theme. 'I could take on another man's child. If I loved the woman, Claudine, it wouldn't matter...nothing would matter! And as a matter of fact I do love a woman...'

There came a point when enough was enough and Tess was way past that point. With a keening sob aching to escape her tight throat, she turned, picked up Ben and ran. She didn't stop until she ran slap bang into a tall figure dressed in an exquisitely cut dark suit that shrieked of expensive bespoke tailoring.

She placed a soothing hand on Ben's head as he stirred in his sleep. Wiping the moisture from her cheeks, she lifted her downcast head to mumble an apology to the stranger.

Her tragic tear-washed eyes seemed to fill her entire face. She summoned a weak smile.

'I'm sorry... Oh, it's you!'

'Good afternoon, Miss Trelawny.' Edgar Farrar's gaze slid from her tear-stained face to the child asleep in her arms.

'He's got Alec's colouring,' came the terse verdict after a moment of intense, apparently unemotional scrutiny.

Eyes wide and fearful, Tess took an automatic step backwards.

A sneer appeared on his lined, lean face. 'Don't worry, child, I'm not about to snatch him away.'

Tess wasn't too keen on playing Little Red Riding Hood to his big bad wolf. Her mouth firmed as she looked him straight in the eyes and declared in a clear voice, 'I wouldn't let you.' She didn't want him having any doubts on that score.

'No, I don't suppose you would.' A thoughtful expression accompanied this response. 'Is Rafe at home?'

At the mention of Rafe she was plunged straight back into the depths of despair.

'He's got company.'

Edgar hadn't mentioned her tears, but it was unrealistic to suppose he hadn't noticed and put two and two together. His next words confirmed her suspicions and his interrogator's keen eye.

'The sort of company that makes you weep?' With a lordly gesture he brushed aside Tess's mechanical rebuttal. 'You don't strike me as a young woman who weeps easily'

Another second and he'd see exactly how easily she could weep. 'If you'll excuse me.' She tried to brush past him but he moved to block her path.

'No, I don't think I will.'

'Pardon?'

'I won't excuse you just yet. Where exactly are you going?'

It was easier to reply than argue, so she did. 'I'm going to catch the first train home.'

A crowded train on a hot and sticky day—what better way to round off a perfect day? she wondered sourly. What was I thinking of, imagining even for one minute that Rafe might admit he felt anything other than lust, and possibly pity for me? She flinched away from the mortification of her own stupidity. At least she'd had her eyes opened before she'd made a total fool of herself…the thought of her lucky escape didn't do much to improve her frame of mind.

'I think we can do rather better than the train.'

Edgar moved—quite nimbly for someone of his years—to one side and Tess saw the large sleek Rolls illegally parked at the kerbside.

At a gesture from the owner the driver leapt out and opened the nearside passenger door. She glanced nervously over her shoulder, half expecting Rafe or his lover to emerge from the building. Deliverance had never looked so fraught with danger to Tess, or so luxurious.

She didn't imagine for one moment that Edgar's gesture had been motivated by concern for her welfare. On the one hand her nose was detecting the unmistakable odour of an ulterior motive, but on the other there was no denying that railway travel with a tired toddler was no picnic, especially when you'd been stupid enough to leave behind all the toddler's favourite foods and toys. She wanted to be well clear of here when Rafe discovered the bag of baby things in his bedroom.

'I thought you were going to see Rafe.'

The elder Farrar didn't deny this. 'As were you…' her determined rescuer pointed out.

'I changed my mind.' About a lot of things.

'Not the sole prerogative of women. Now get in, Miss Trelawny…' his shrewd eyes scanned her pale face '…this is becoming tiresome.'

What was it about the Farrar men that made them automatically assume she was there for them to bully?

'I should explain that I react very negatively to intimidation tactics.'

'The last time we spoke you were far more decisive. Despite what you might have been told, I don't eat babies.' He gave a thin-lipped smile.

'I suppose,' she conceded ungraciously, 'that you're the lesser of two evils.' Actually it was the realisation that her wallet had been in the holdall along with Ben's things that tipped the balance. She sat back in the air-conditioned luxury and sighed.

'Would I be correct in assuming that the greater evil is tall, dark and at present entertaining another woman?'

It would seem that Rafe had inherited his irritating habit of reading between the lines from his father. Aware that she was being observed for any response, Tess willed her expression to remain impassive.

'We'll be going home, William,' her host told the driver.

'You'll be happy to know the wedding won't be going ahead.' Somehow she didn't think that Rafe was going to be too sad when she explained she could no longer consider marrying him.

If this news gladdened the elderly financier's heart, he hid it well. 'You know, you look very like your grandmother.'

Tess was momentarily diverted from the gloomy contemplation of the rest of her life. 'I didn't know you knew Gran.'

'A remarkable woman. When it came to my attention that Rafe was making nocturnal visits to your home, I confronted her.'

'You knew!'

'So did your grandmother. She assured me that when the time was right she'd put a stop to it. I trusted her judgement.'

'Put a stop…' Tess puzzled.

'I believe she had a word with Rafe when she considered it to be inappropriate.'

'Oh! I didn't know…' Tess's cheeks began to burn. 'It was all perfectly innocent!' she protested.

'I never doubted it, but youthful hormones being what they are…' He gave an expressive shrug. 'Actually, I was glad that there was somewhere that Rafe felt at home.'

The expression on his hard, autocratic face hadn't altered,

but something in his tone made Tess forget her own embarrassment and stare.

'You knew Rafe was unhappy, yet you didn't do anything about it,' she accused.

'My hands were tied,' he told her stiffly. 'I regretted it, but...'

'Your regret didn't do Rafe much good,' she told him bluntly. 'The way I see it, he suffered for your mistakes!'

'It seems to me that Rafe is most fortunate to have so loyal a friend.'

'I don't want to be his *friend*!' she wailed. 'Oh, God!' She gulped, covering her mouth with her hand. 'I'm sorry.' She sniffed and found a large, beautifully laundered white handkerchief thrust in her hand.

'I was under the impression that Rafe desired more too,' Rafe's father murmured drily.

'That was all an act,' she admitted miserably.

'My, my, the boy's talents are limitless, it would seem. You probably think I was extremely...*clumsy* when I told Rafe about his true parentage.'

'I think your timing was a bit off, say by twenty years or so,' she told him resentfully.

'I loved Natalie, you know.' He glowered at a startled Tess as if she was about to dispute this surprising confession.

'I don't really remember her. Rafe has a photo...' Rafe had inherited her dark colouring.

'You'll find as you get older that there are pivotal moments in life. You don't always recognise those decisions for what they are at the time. You don't realise there's no going back... There are so many things I'd do differently, though loving Natalie is not one of them,' he growled. 'There hasn't been a day since she left I haven't wished I'd had the guts to create a scandal and say to hell with family honour! I shouldn't have sent her away, we should have gone with her, the boy and I…but it's too late now. Do you think me a very selfish man?' he wondered.

There was an intensely sad expression in Edgar's pale blue eyes as he contemplated what might have been. Tess felt some of her hostility dissolve towards this powerful, driven old man.

'I suppose it makes me think of you as human…which I have to admit,' she told him with a tiny spurt of mischief, 'comes as something of a surprise to me.' Her expression sobered. 'Have you explained to Rafe how you felt about his mother? It might help.'

The old man's dark scowl was back. 'I tried…you heard me…Rafe isn't interested in listening.'

'Since when did you take no for an answer? Not that it's any of my business,' she added, uncomfortably aware that, just when she ought to be distancing herself from the Farrars, she was getting sucked in all over again.

'While you're bringing up the youngest Farrar—and, if I may say so, doing an excellent job of it…' this unexpected commendation stilled her alarmed protest '…I would think that it's as much your business as anyone's.'

'Does that mean…?'

'Give me some credit! I'm stubborn, girl, not blind! I can see that you're an excellent mother to the boy. I would, however, like to get to know my great-grandson. How do you feel about that?'

'If you must know, relieved.'

'Excellent! Then, if you're not too tired, why not bring Ben here over…he does wake up occasionally, I take it?'

'Oh, he wakes up, all right,' Tess promised drily.

'Bring him over to the house for afternoon tea. I'll send the car for you. It would be an opportunity for us to discuss financial arrangements.'

The smile vanished from Tess's face. That would teach her to remember not to lower her defences with a Farrar. 'I don't want your money.'

Regarding the mutinous jut of her soft chin with a thoughtful expression, Edgar leaned forward in his seat and spoke softly.

'I've never been a big fan of this modern compromise nonsense either, but then look where stiff-necked pride has got me... I'm a lonely old man with one son who would stab me in the back for my money, if he thought he could get away with it, and another who hates my guts and wouldn't take my hand if he was drowning. Let me do something for Ben, Tess?'

Despite her natural inclination to view everything he said with cynicism and hostility, she was impressed by his obvious sincerity. Even allowing for the fact the 'lonely old man' part was a little bit hard to swallow, Tess was sure that this was as close to pleading as Edgar Farrar had ever been and it was close enough to amaze her.

'We'd like to come to tea.'

It wasn't a major concession, but to judge by Edgar's expression he was satisfied with his progress.

'You mentioned that you're no longer engaged to my son...'

Her spine stiffened until her back was barely brushing the deep upholstery. 'That's right.'

'Did you come to this conclusion as a couple, or was this a unilateral decision... *your* unilateral decision?'

'Rafe won't fight me on this,' she assured him dully.

'If you're sure...? You accused me earlier of not taking no for an answer. I think you'll find when it comes to obstinacy Rafe is in a class of his own. Think about it,' he advised when she didn't respond.

Tess was treated to a first-hand sample of Rafe's stubbornness later that day when she'd secured a freshly scrubbed and refreshed Ben in the back of the chauffeur-driven Rolls and was sliding in beside him.

'Where the hell do you think you're going?'

She slammed the door in Rafe's face. 'Drive on, please!' Tess appealed to the impassive-faced driver.

'Don't move!' Rafe barked, banging his hand on the roof of the Rolls and poking his head through the open rear window.

The driver was obviously at a loss to know what to make of his conflicting instructions. Rafe took advantage of his indecision.

'You do know who this car belongs to, don't you?'

'I'd hardly get into a stranger's car, would I?' she announced carelessly.

'I've not even been gone forty-eight hours. You've got to hand it to the old man, he's a fast worker.' He sounded anything but admiring. 'How did he work the magic? A slick line or have I misjudged you—did it just take a nice fat cheque?' he jeered nastily.

'If I didn't know it would frighten Ben,' she snapped, glancing protectively towards the small boy fastened into his brand-new child restraint before bestowing a contemptuous glare on Rafe, 'I'd slap that self-righteous smirk off your face.'

It was the fact she obviously considered he could be a threat to Ben rather than the threat of physical violence that really made him mad!

'Would you care to explain to me exactly what's going on? I found your bag complete with credit cards, cash and cheque-book on my bed. You, however, were noticeable by your absence. You haven't been answering my calls—as far as I knew you could have been lying on a morgue slab!' He bowed his dark head and she saw his knuckles whiten against the window rim.

'Don't be so dramatic!' she advised him scornfully.

His head lifted sharply; his dark eyes were burning. 'I've been *frantic*!'

Tess sniffed with deliberate disdain, but her feelings overcame her.

'Was that before or after you'd finished rolling around on the bed with Claudine?' she spat, abandoning her dignified contempt in favour of green-eyed—in more ways than one—fury!

Was there no end to his deceit? she wondered, conveniently ignoring the fact he'd never denied being in love with Claudine as she viewed with growing contempt his superb display of bewildered confusion.

'Will you please drive on?' she pleaded urgently.

Her desperation must have swung the day because the driver managed to overcome his reluctance to leave his employer's heir standing ignominiously at the side of the road and started up the engine.

Tess had a last glimpse of Rafe's furious features just before the car drew away. Her sigh of relief turned out to be premature; the car was still gathering speed when the door beside her was yanked open and Rafe almost landed on top of her.

'How dare you?' she gasped, putting as much space between her and Rafe as was humanly possible given the confined area—the confined part was already inflicting major damage to her nervous system! Her senses were so finely tuned to him that the barely detectable male scent that emanated from his warm, lean body made her stomach muscles go into a series of seriously disturbing spasms. A wave of sexual longing so powerful it literally robbed her of breath for several terrifying moments swept through her.

He grinned coldly through gritted teeth. 'There are few things I don't dare when it comes to getting what I want.'

And am I supposed to believe that's me? 'What am I supposed to do now...applaud?' She dealt him a look of withering scorn. 'Go flex your ego somewhere else!' She raised her voice. 'Will you stop the car, please? Mr Farrar is getting out.'

'Actually,' Rafe drawled, 'I'm not. Short of physical

force, angel, what do you suppose you can do about that?' He smiled with grim satisfaction.

He had her there and they both knew it. The chauffeur didn't look able or willing to eject Rafe, and, considering the dangerous light in his eyes, she didn't altogether blame him.

'That was such a stupid, dangerous thing to do, you could have slipped and...' Her scolding tone faded as an image of Rafe under the wheels of a moving vehicle popped into her head. She had to close her eyes until the waves of nausea passed.

'Are you all right?'

Tess felt his hand on her shoulder. His arm lightly grazed her breasts, which had been curiously tender of late. The contact made her nipples burn; she winced and pulled away.

'So now you can't stand me to touch you!' he thundered in an outraged voice that suggested he'd do his utmost to make her retract it if she was foolish enough to confirm this accusation.

Tess opened her mouth to contradict him when it occurred to her that she'd be better off letting this false impression stand, though, she reflected bitterly, he couldn't be nearly as intelligent as everyone thought he was if he could think she didn't like his touch... It was weak, it was pathetic, but she was dying inside for his touch!

Head on one side, she subjected his sternly handsome face to an apparently objective scrutiny. 'Sulky doesn't suit you,' she concluded after a short silence.

'I'll try and remember that,' he promised grimly.

'What's your next trick going to be?' she rounded on him with brittle sarcasm. 'Wing-walking or jumping from a ten-storey building? I know all *little boys* like to pretend they're James Bond.' She gave a superior smile as he coloured self-consciously. 'But I'd be grateful if you could restrain yourself while Ben is watching. He tries to ape everything you do—for some reason he thinks you're marvellous.'

'And you don't?'

'I think you're...' She took a steadying breath. 'I won't repeat in front of Ben what I think of you.'

Rafe tore his unresponsive eyes from the heaving surge of her bosom. 'This isn't about that damned announcement, is it?'

'Oh, you're so quick,' she admired. 'No, it isn't about the announcement, which, incidentally, you'd better retract. It's about the fact you met up with Claudine and told her you still loved her.'

'*I what?*'

'Don't bother denying it! I heard you.'

'You heard?'

'Yes, I heard. For a man who makes his living asking questions, you sound like a parrot.'

The driver pulled the car over onto the grass verge as they finally cleared the section of hairpin bends in the road. He cleared his throat discreetly.

'Will this do, miss, for Mr Farrar to get out...?'

'Mr Farrar isn't getting out,' Rafe contradicted flatly.

'Fine, then we are.' Her trembling fingers were making heavy weather of the baby harness. 'I'll walk.'

Rafe sat for a moment watching the slender, rigid-backed figure stalk along the road ahead. He sighed.

'Thanks, we'll *all* walk.'

'What shall I tell the other Mr Farrar?' the driver yelled worriedly after Rafe.

'Don't tempt me,' Rafe muttered as he broke into a jog to catch up with Tess. 'Slow down, woman. Let me carry Ben.'

'We can manage without you.'

'Maybe you can, but I sure as hell can't manage without you,' Rafe ground back forcefully.

Tess tried to blink back the tears and almost tripped over. Forced to come to a halt—there was no way she was outrunning him—she kissed the top of Ben's head apologetically.

'Why are you saying this to me?' she asked in an agonised whisper. 'Why are you being so cruel? There's no need to pretend any more. I know how you feel—'

His bitter laugh cut her off. 'If that wasn't so tragic it would be funny!'

Bewildered by the biting note in his acrid observation, Tess didn't put up much of a fight when he took her hand and drew her off the road and into a small grassy picnic area. The car, which had been crawling along behind them, came to a full stop several yards away.

'Edgar isn't going to try and take Ben off me.'

'I don't know or care just now how you happened to get cosy with *Edgar* all of a sudden.' He proceeded to take Ben from her. 'You play here, mate,' he said, putting him down on the floor.

Ben appeared perfectly willing to co-operate with the big man who made him laugh.

'*Now...!*' Grim determination was etched in every intriguing plane and hollow of his tense, lean face.

'Don't use that tone with me!'

'You're not leaving here until you tell me what the hell you're talking about.'

'You're in love with Claudine and you don't care if her baby isn't yours.'

Comprehension flickered into his eyes. 'So *that's* what you heard.'

Her shoulders sagged. One tiny part of her had still been hoping against all the odds that there would be some sort of last-minute reprieve. No wonder he sounded so relieved— he was probably just grateful he no longer had the onerous task of explaining the state of play to her.

'Are you going to wish me well?' He might have bent down to add a stick to Ben's growing collection, but his watchful regard was still reserved for Tess.

Tess knew she'd bite off her tongue before she could bring herself to mouth meaningless platitudes—if that made her a sore loser, so be it!

'I just hope you know what you're doing. I hope you'll forgive me for talking frankly,' she said earnestly, 'but we've been friends for a long time and I...I...care about you...' she mumbled.

He rose to his feet and her stoic, pain-filled gaze slid uncomfortably away from his alert glance.

'That's nice,' he said softly, taking her chin in one hand. 'How much?' he asked huskily, tilting her face up to him.

Rafe's face was a dark silhouette as she squinted against the strong early evening sun. 'How much what?' she whispered.

'How much do you care about me?' His fingers trailed down her cheek as, eyes wild with panic, she tore herself free.

'Ben, Ben...' She suddenly developed an uncharacteristic concern about the grass stains on his clean pale blue shirt. 'You little grub!' she chided softly. 'And look at your hands,' she fussed, bending down to turn over his chubby little baby hands.

'Leave him be, Tess, there's no harm in a little dirt.' Firmly Rafe took possession of her own hands and pulled her to her feet. 'You didn't answer me,' he reminded her, running a finger down the curve of her cheek.

'That wasn't an accident.' Her mouth wouldn't form the smile to accompany her flippant response. 'What do you want me to say?' she asked him angrily.

'I want you to say that you've been enduring seven kinds of hell since you *discovered* I'm so besotted I'd even take on another man's child...that the obstacle hasn't been created that could stop me loving my woman! I want to hear that I'm not the only one who's been suffering. *You little fool!*' he groaned hoarsely as he hauled her unceremoniously into his strong arms and kissed her.

It was the sort of kiss that went on for a long, *long* time. She emerged panting hard, one shaking hand on her heaving bosom. Ears filled with the pounding of her heartbeat, she stepped back a pace and struggled to gather her fatally scattered thoughts.

A deep frown puckered her smooth brow; her head spun. 'It felt like you meant that.' Which meant what, exactly...?

He grinned tautly in response to her breathless observation.

'Did you come up to town because you wanted to spy on me?' His blazing eyes held the definite suggestion he'd go to any lengths to extract a reply.

She could still feel the sensuous impression of his warm lips on her tender mouth, still taste him; preserving her pride no longer seemed particularly important.

Pretending that they could go back to their old cosy relationship was obviously a non-starter, and why should she be ashamed of loving him anyhow? It wasn't as if things could get more strained or awkward than they already were!

Bravely she lifted her head and tossed back her hair. 'I felt guilty because I was marrying you under false pretences. I didn't want to marry you because of Ben, I wanted to marry you because I'm in love with you. When I overheard...' Her brave voice faltered and she bit her quivering lip. 'I realised there wasn't much point. Why did you kiss me like that, Rafe?'

'Like I couldn't get enough of you?' He continued in the same hard, driven tone, his eyes boring mercilessly into her. 'Like you're as essential as oxygen? Like you're just as intoxicating as a twenty-year-old bottle of fine brandy? Like I want a Tess hangover for the rest of my life? Like you're the woman I love enough to marry no matter what?' His voice dropped with each successive question until it was a deep, impossibly sexy growl which made her receptive pulses leap crazily.

It finally clicked! And with a great leap of faith Tess

stepped off the precipice that had opened at her feet with a smile on her lips. Joy imploded in her head.

'Even if *I* was carrying another man's child!' She gasped, raising shining eyes to his face.

'I knew you'd get there eventually,' he drawled. 'Claudine got the point I was trying to make straight off.'

'Oh, I wish I could, Rafe!' Tess sighed.

His eyes were impossibly tender. 'Wish you could have another man's child?' he teased softly.

Her eyelashes fluttered protectively downwards. 'No, I wish I could carry yours,' she explained gruffly.

'Look at me!' She'd never heard Rafe use that precise tone before; she responded to the command without thinking. His eyes bored down into hers. 'I don't want to hear you talk like that ever *ever* again. I've got you, that's all I need. I have got you, haven't I?'

She could hardly believe that Rafe was seeking reassurance from her! The troubled expression faded from her face as she vigorously nodded. With a grin on her face, she opened her arms wide.

'I'm all yours!' she carolled.

A fierce grin split his lean features. 'Hold that thought for a more private occasion,' he pleaded with a groan.

She shook her head in blissful bemusement. 'You were talking about loving *me*, not...' Self-consciously she stopped, unable to bring herself to say the name of the other woman.

'Not Claudine,' he said it for her. Gathering her face tenderly between his hands as he did so. 'Never Claudine. She was always acting a part—the Claudine I convinced myself I loved never even existed. She turned up uninvited on my doorstep today and I didn't feel a thing. After living with the real thing I've lost my taste for insipid imitations.' His eyes were fiercely tender as they drank in her lovestruck features. 'You're simply, superbly *amazing*,' he choked huskily.

'I am?' The imbecilic grin just wouldn't budge from her face, but Rafe didn't seem to mind. 'It must have come as a shock to her,' Tess intoned piously, while struggling to suppress an unladylike urge to punch the air triumphantly.

'She had her chance,' Rafe murmured heartlessly. 'Lucky for me she didn't take it. Hell would be falling in love with you and not being able to do anything about it.'

'Well, you can do something about it,' she promised, smiling blissfully. 'You can do anything you like.'

'You know what I like,' he growled, drawing her close. She shivered as his lips moved sensuously over the sweet curve of her neck. He pressed his mouth to her ear. 'I like,' his dark, wicked whisper explained, 'finding you wet and warm every time I touch you. Every time you pushed me away I reminded myself of that.'

Her legs sagged, and she whimpered as a wave of longing almost washed her away. She clung to him. 'I never pushed you away.'

'Not physically.'

She buried her head against his shoulder. 'This must be a dream.'

Rafe tilted her head firmly up to him. 'Oh, no, angel, this is the real thing,' he contradicted firmly.

'I've been so naggy and horrible,' she fretted.

'It's called frustration, angel. The sooner we get married, the better.'

A loud baby chuckle came from the ground beside them.

Laughing, they both looked down. 'That settles it!' Rafe announced. 'The baby has the clinching vote.'

'Let's just call it a unanimous decision,' Tess suggested happily.

CHAPTER TEN

WITH Ben between them they strolled towards the big house. To Tess, who was seeing things with the benefit of love-enhanced vision, the mellow stone facade seemed to be smiling benignly down at them.

'There's Edgar,' she said, spotting a tall figure beside the reed-edged lake. She lifted her hand in greeting. 'Now be nice,' she admonished sternly.

'I'm hurt you think me capable of being anything else.'

She threw him an exasperated, but loving glance. 'And don't sneer,' she instructed, lifting her hand to coax his curling lip back in place. 'Let's go and meet him halfway.'

'Subtle symbolism.'

'I thought you were going to be nice?'

'Nag…nag…' Rafe kissed her conveniently placed finger, drawing it into his mouth; his eyes darkened with male satisfaction when he saw the tell-tale tide of heat travel over her exposed skin.

'I'm serious, Rafe!' she told him hoarsely as she snatched her hand away.

'Angel, for you I'd have tea with the devil himself.'

'The way you were going on I thought we were.'

They were only a hundred yards or so away from Rafe's father when there was a loud creak followed by a sickening groan as the hand-rail on the far side of the old wooden bridge that was suspended across the narrow end of the lake broke off and landed in the lake with a loud splash. They watched in horror as it took Edgar with it.

'Hell!' Rafe hit the ground at a flat-out run.

Hampered by Ben, Tess was much slower. By the time

she reached the reed-choked bank of the lake, Edgar was crawling out of the muddy shallows.

She bent down beside him. 'Are you all right?'

Edgar dragged an unsteady hand through his sodden head of silvered hair. 'I always meant to learn to swim.' He looked around. 'Where's the boy?'

At first Tess thought he meant Ben, who seemed interested rather than distressed by the unexpected turn of events. Then she realised who he was looking for.

'Rafe!' she yelled out loudly as panic and alarm began to set in seriously. 'Rafe, where are you?'

'He was right beside me in the water until we got to the shallows.' Edgar staggered to his feet and, eyes shaded with his hand, looked out at the still, silent water.

The intense coldness started on the inside and worked its way outwards until Tess felt like a solid block of ice. 'No, this isn't happening!' she mumbled indistinctly from between bluish lips. Desperately she continued to call his name.

'Watch Ben!' she told the shivering and shocked figure beside her. 'Don't let him near the water!'

Tears were running unchecked down her cheeks as she ran towards the water's edge and began to wade in. Later she wouldn't be able to recall the exact sequence of events that led to her being thigh-deep in the inhospitable lake, her voice hoarse from crying his name.

'Please let him be all right, please let him be all right!' she repeated like a mantra. 'So help me, Rafe, if you do this to me I'll never forgive you,' she yelled out. 'Do you hear me? *Never!*'

'I hear you.'

With a cry she spun around in the direction of the voice and he was standing there looking pretty terrible, with a deep, gaping gash that began at cheekbone-level and disappeared into his hairline. Dizzying relief hit in a vast tidal wave. Terrible didn't matter—he was in one piece. He was alive!

'Tess...Tess...?' She could hear her name being repeated over and over with some urgency, then the darkness closed in. She didn't hear or see anything else until some time later.

'Where am I?' Part of her brain proceeded to supply her with the necessary information while the other part cringed at the corny predictability of her question.

'In hospital!'

'*Rafe?*' With a gasp she pulled herself into a sitting position.

The white-coated figure pushed her back down. 'Your companions are fine. The elder Mr Farrar was in the middle of discharging himself the last time I saw him, the little chap is with him. The gash on your other friend's head required stitches.'

'How did he...?'

'He collided with a submerged piece of bridge apparently and was dazed. We'll keep him in overnight just to be on the safe side, but he'll be fine.'

'What's wrong with me?'

'Been feeling a bit off colour lately, have we?' came the cagey response.

'I don't know about you,' she responded testily, 'but I have. Sorry,' she added, ashamed of her churlish response. The man was only trying to help her, she reminded herself.

The medic stopped being enigmatic and told her. She didn't believe him; she didn't believe quite loudly. But when he performed the tests to confirm his diagnosis she had no choice but to accept what he was saying was true. It wasn't easy—miracles never were easy to believe.

She was still lying there in a state of euphoric shock when the door opened. She sighed—not again. Had the staff here never heard of neglect? If she had her blood pressure taken once more she'd scream—Tess wasn't the best patient in the world.

The scowl faded from her face when she saw who it was. Greedily her eyes drank in the details of his bruised and battered but beloved face.

'Well, don't just lie there, move over, woman,' her grumpy lover mumbled.

'They,' she predicted, meaning the uniformed medical types who were far too bossy for her taste, 'won't like it.' The possibility of their disapproval didn't stop her throwing open the covers invitingly and shuffling to one side.

'I don't give a damn what they like,' Rafe muttered, displaying an arrogant disregard for the wishes of the medical establishment.

'They'll make you leave.' She snuggled closer and discovered that under the badly fitting hospital-issue dressing gown Rafe was wearing a thin cotton gown like her own that was open to the elements—or, in this case, her questing hands—all the way down the back.

'Not if they don't find me. Innovators are never appreciated,' he mourned. 'I'm a fearless pioneer of the bed-sharing scheme.'

'Your poor, poor face,' she crooned gently, touching the bruised side of his face tenderly. 'Talking about fear, don't ever, *ever* do that to me again!' Her eyes darkened as the memory of those awful few moments when she'd thought she'd lost him for ever surfaced once more. 'I think I've accumulated enough material to keep my nightmares supplied for the foreseeable future.'

'Poor baby, I'm sorry. If we're talking fear...' He drew a ragged breath and pulled her head down onto his chest. Tess lay there, content to hear the steady thud of his heartbeat. 'When you collapsed like that I went totally to pieces. If it hadn't been for Edgar I might still be standing there with you in my arms like a great useless lump of wood!' His uneven voice was laden with bitter self-recrimination.

'Remind me to thank him,' she said, arranging her curvy bits with catlike pleasure around his hard masculine frame, a frame which didn't feel any the worse for his experience.

'I already did; in the ambulance after you came to.'

Tess, who had been diverted by the promising news that Rafe had actually been speaking with his father, lifted her head abruptly. 'I came to?'

'Don't you remember?' He smoothed down her feathery dark brows with the square tip of his thumb.

'I just remember waking up here.'

'But you are all right? What did the doctor say?'

She could almost feel his alarm growing. 'I'm fine...'

'I can hear a but, Tess.' He took her jaw between thumb and forefinger and left her with no choice but to meet his interrogative gaze. 'I thought we'd done with secrets, but I can see them in your eyes,' he reproached.

'It might be inconvenient having a husband who can read me so well.'

He ignored her weak attempt at levity. 'So I'm right; something is wrong.'

'Not *wrong*, exactly...at least, I hope you won't think so...I don't...but I suppose it depends...'

He placed a gentle but firm finger to her lips. 'You're babbling.'

'You know how I told you I can't have babies.'

Compassion was swiftly replaced by determination in his eyes. 'It doesn't matter. I want you, not babies.'

'What if we come as a package deal?'

The hand that was massaging her scalp through the dense covering of shiny hair stilled suddenly; his expression froze mid-smile.

'Are you trying to tell me...?'

Tess nodded vigorously. 'I'm pregnant.' It felt strange thinking it; saying it was proving to be an even more wonderfully peculiar experience.

'You can't be.'

'That's what I said,' she agreed. 'But they did all the tests, I even saw the heartbeat on the scan...' The special memory brought a sheen of emotional tears to her wide, wondering eyes. 'Apparently there's all the difference in the world between impossible and improbable. They explained it all scientifically, but I still think it's a miracle,' she announced, a dreamy expression of wonder drifting once more across her face. 'I had all the symptoms, but it just didn't occur to me...'

The glazed expression faded from his face as he grinned. It was possibly the least intelligent expression she'd ever seen on his lean face, and perhaps the most satisfying. She'd thought he'd be happy, but it was good to have it confirmed.

'We're going to have a baby, Tess.' He sounded incredibly complacent about the fact.

'I know, darling.'

'A brother for Ben...'

'Or a sister,' she felt impelled to add.

'Whatever,' he agreed with vague good humour. He gave a sudden whoop of unrestrained joy and sat up. Eyes burning with a stunned kind of enthusiasm, he planted his hands on the pillow and leaned anxiously over her.

'Is everything all right? Are you...? Is there anything you should be doing...resting...?'

'This is resting, Rafe,' she pointed out. 'And I've been given a complete clean bill of health by the doctor. So you can relax.'

'Do you think the baby would mind if I kiss you?'

'I've not the foggiest, but I'd mind very much if you didn't,' she announced firmly.

The nurse continued to stare at the crumpled bed. 'He should be here,' she said for the fourth time.

'You mean you've *lost* my son?' The notion of his six-feet-four son being mislaid made Edgar's lips twitch. He had his own ideas about where the boy was.

'Well, not *lost*, exactly…we just don't know where he is,' she admitted miserably.

'A fine distinction, the significance of which escapes me at the moment.'

'He can't have gone far; he doesn't have any clothes. People with head injuries can sometimes do unpredictable things,' she admitted unhappily.

'I feel very much better knowing that.' His stern expression faded. 'Don't worry too much, we used to lose him all the time when he was a boy. Do you mind telling me where Miss Trelawny's room is? I take it Miss Trelawny is in her room, not wandering around…?'

'I don't know if Miss Trelawny is allowed visitors. I'll check…' Two seconds' exposure to the hard Farrar glare and her uncertainty had the good sense to vanish. 'I'll show you straight away, sir.'

'I thought so!' Edgar, pleased to have his hunch proved right, boomed as the door to Tess's small room opened.

'Oh, dear!' the nurse beside him gasped in a scandalised tone as she stared in disbelief at the two figures entwined on the narrow hospital-issue bed. 'You can't do that sort of thing here.'

'I think a little flexibility is called for here,' Edgar announced authoritatively. 'It's not as if they're having an orgy or anything. Stands to reason, the boy's in pain.'

'Not that much pain,' Rafe responded in defence of his libido.

Tess choked and pulled the covers over her head.

'Besides, it would be useless telling him he can't share her bed, my dear, he's been crawling into it since he was fourteen years old.'

'Thirteen,' Rafe corrected with an appreciative gleam in his eyes.

'I don't think you'll ever break him of the habit. Nor,' Edgar added, his eyes gravely holding Rafe's, 'would I want to.'

'Tell her I'll keep an eye on Ben tonight,' she heard Edgar say in a loud voice, for all the world as if she'd left the room. 'She's not to worry.'

'I will,' Rafe promised, with a quiver in his voice as Tess viciously pinched the non-existent spare flesh across his belly. 'Would you mind feeding the dog too?'

'Have they gone?' Tess asked after the room had gone quiet.

Rafe lifted the covers. 'It's safe, you can come out now. I'd have joined you, but I thought it wiser not to invite smutty speculation.'

Tess gave a horrified croak and emerged, her hot cheeks glowing and her hair wildly tangled. 'They didn't think I was...?' she began in a horrified whisper, then she saw the devilish laughter dancing in his dark eyes. She swatted playfully at his chest. 'You rat! Did you see that girl's face!' she groaned.

'Why would I look at another woman when you're around?'

'I'd prefer it if you restricted your *looking* to a minimum when I'm not around too. How could Edgar say those things? And you egged him on,' she accused indignantly.

'Actually I thought he was talking a lot of sense. Perhaps I will invite him to our wedding after all,' he mused thoughtfully.

'Well, if he doesn't come neither do I.'

'In that case, angel, he's top of the list.' The covers muffled her giggles and anxious squeals of protest as he pulled the covers over both their heads.

'It looked interesting when you did it...I was wondering...'

'Rafe, you can't do *that*!'

She rapidly discovered that Rafe *could* do that! Being Rafe, he did it very well indeed.

VIVA LA VIDA DE AMOR!

They speak the language of passion.

In Harlequin Presents®,
you'll find a special kind of
lover—full of Latin charm.
Whether he's relaxing in denims,
or dressed for dinner, giving
you diamonds, or simply sweet
dreams, he's got spirit,
style and sex appeal!

LATIN LOVERS

is the new miniseries from
Harlequin Presents® for anyone
who enjoys hot romance!

July 2001
HER SECRET BRIDEGROOM
#2191
by Kate Walker

September 2001
DUARTE'S CHILD #2199
by Lynne Graham

November 2001
A SPANISH AFFAIR #2213
by Helen Brooks

Available wherever
Harlequin books are sold.

Visit us at www.eHarlequin.com
HPLL

*Harlequin invites you
to walk down the aisle . . .*

To honor our year long celebration of weddings, we are offering an exciting opportunity for you to own the Harlequin Bride Doll. Handcrafted in fine bisque porcelain, the wedding doll is dressed for her wedding day in a cream satin gown accented by lace trim. She carries an exquisite traditional bridal bouquet and wears a cathedral-length dotted Swiss veil. Embroidered flowers cascade down her lace overskirt to the scalloped hemline; underneath all is a multi-layered crinoline.

Join us in our celebration of weddings by sending away for your own Harlequin Bride Doll. This doll regularly retails for $74.95 U.S./approx. $108.68 CDN. One doll per household. Requests must be received no later than December 31, 2001. Offer good while quantities of gifts last. Please allow 6-8 weeks for delivery. Offer good in the U.S. and Canada only. Become part of this exciting offer!

**Simply complete the order form and mail to:
"A Walk Down the Aisle"**

IN U.S.A
P.O. Box 9057
3010 Walden Ave.
Buffalo, NY 14269-9057

IN CANADA
P.O. Box 622
Fort Erie, Ontario
L2A 5X3

Enclosed are eight (8) proofs of purchase found in the last pages of every specially marked Harlequin series book and $3.75 check or money order (for postage and handling). Please send my Harlequin Bride Doll to:

Name (PLEASE PRINT)

Address   Apt. #

City   State/Prov.   Zip/Postal Code

Account # (if applicable)   **097 KIK DAEW**

HARLEQUIN®
Makes any time special ®

Visit us at www.eHarlequin.com

A Walk Down the Aisle
Free Bride Doll Offer
One Proof-of-Purchase

PHWDAPOPR2

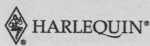

HARLEQUIN®

makes any time special—online...

eHARLEQUIN.com

your romantic life

—Romance 101—
♥ Guides to romance, dating and flirting.

—Dr. Romance —
♥ Get romance advice and tips from our expert, Dr. Romance.

—Recipes for Romance —
♥ How to plan romantic meals for you and your sweetie.

—Daily Love Dose—
♥ Tips on how to keep the romance alive every day.

—Tales from the Heart—
♥ Discuss romantic dilemmas with other members in our Tales from the Heart message board.

All this and more available at
www.eHarlequin.com
on Women.com Networks

HINTL1R

Three of your favorite authors will move you to tears
and laughter in three wonderfully emotional stories,
bringing you…

Mistletoe Miracles

A brand-new anthology from

BETTY NEELS
CATHERINE GEORGE
MARION LENNOX

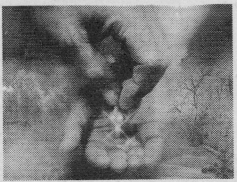

The warmth and magic of the holiday season comes alive
in this collection in which three couples learn that
Christmas is a time when miracles really *do* come true.

Available in November 2001 at your favorite retail outlet.

HARLEQUIN®
Makes any time special ®

Visit us at www.eHarlequin.com

PHMBC

*Together for the first time
in one Collector's Edition!*

New York Times bestselling authors

Barbara Delinsky

Catherine Coulter

Linda Howard

Forever Yours

**A special trade-size volume containing three
complete novels that showcase the passion,
imagination and stunning power that these
talented authors are famous for.**

Coming to your favorite retail outlet in December 2001.

HARLEQUIN®
Makes any time special ®

Visit us at www.eHarlequin.com

PHFY

HARLEQUIN Presents
Passion™

Looking for stories that **sizzle?**

Wanting a read that has a little extra **spice?**

Harlequin Presents® is thrilled to bring
you romances that turn up the **heat!**

Every other month there'll be a
PRESENTS PASSION™
book by one of your favorite authors.

Don't miss...
CHRISTOS'S PROMISE
by **Jane Porter**
On sale October 2001, Harlequin Presents® #2210

Pick up a **PRESENTS PASSION™**—
where **seduction** is guaranteed!

Available wherever Harlequin books are sold.

HARLEQUIN®
Makes any time special ®

Visit us at www.eHarlequin.com   HPSEPASS

If you enjoyed what you just read,
then we've got an offer you can't resist!

Take 2 bestselling love stories FREE!

Plus get a FREE surprise gift!

Clip this page and mail it to Harlequin Reader Service®

IN U.S.A.	IN CANADA
3010 Walden Ave.	P.O. Box 609
P.O. Box 1867	Fort Erie, Ontario
Buffalo, N.Y. 14240-1867	L2A 5X3

YES! Please send me 2 free Harlequin Presents® novels and my free surprise gift. After receiving them, if I don't wish to receive anymore, I can return the shipping statement marked cancel. If I don't cancel, I will receive 6 brand-new novels every month, before they're available in stores! In the U.S.A., bill me at the bargain price of $3.34 plus 25¢ shipping & handling per book and applicable sales tax, if any*. In Canada, bill me at the bargain price of $3.74 plus 25¢ shipping & handling per book and applicable taxes**. That's the complete price and a savings of at least 10% off the cover prices—what a great deal! I understand that accepting the 2 free books and gift places me under no obligation ever to buy any books. I can always return a shipment and cancel at any time. Even if I never buy another book from Harlequin, the 2 free books and gift are mine to keep forever.

106 HEN DFNY
306 HEN DC7T

Name	(PLEASE PRINT)	
Address	Apt.#	
City	State/Prov.	Zip/Postal Code

* Terms and prices subject to change without notice. Sales tax applicable in N.Y.
** Canadian residents will be charged applicable provincial taxes and GST.
    All orders subject to approval. Offer limited to one per household and not valid to current Harlequin Presents® subscribers..
    ® are registered trademarks of Harlequin Enterprises Limited.

PRES01   ©2001 Harlequin Enterprises Limited

**Lindsay Armstrong...
Helen Bianchin...
Emma Darcy...
Miranda Lee...**

Some of our bestselling writers are Australians!

Look out for their novels about the Wonder from Down Under—where spirited women win the hearts of Australia's most eligible men.

THE **AUSTRALIANS**

Coming soon:
A QUESTION OF MARRIAGE
by Lindsay Armstrong
On sale October 2001, Harlequin Presents® #2208

And look out for:
FUGITIVE BRIDE
by Miranda Lee
On sale November 2001, Harlequin Presents® #2212

Available wherever Harlequin books are sold.

HARLEQUIN®
Makes any time special ®

Visit us at www.eHarlequin.com

HPSEAUS